The Dream Catcher

By Lyndsay Tobiyah

copyright © Lyndsay Tobiyah Coomber 1998

This work is entirely fictitious. Any similarities to events or to persons living are entirely coincidental.

First printed 2007

To contact the author, or for further information please feel free to visit

www.myspace.com/statsinparis

or

http//lyndsaytobiyah.wikidot.com

The author retains all rights to the published content. It may not be reproduced in full or part without prior consent.

ISBN 978-0-9558543-0-9

To love and life, for all of those who care about them

Chapter One

It was incredibly warm. Annie was sitting in the back row of the auditorium. The student anthropology teacher, Matthew Wilkins, was talking about the Mayan temples of Central America, but Annie just could not concentrate. Her mind kept on returning to her dreams. She had had the same dream for three nights running now. Mr. Wilkins was moving on to the Egyptian pyramids, and the similarities their constructions held. But Annie wasn't thinking about them, either, although they looked more like the ones from her dreams than the Mayan temples. She was all ready to close her eyes and drift off to a gentle sleep, when the bell rang loudly above her left ear. The class was excused, and they all moved loudly out of the auditorium. Annie was obviously not in as much of a hurry as the others, as she stayed in her seat, trying to wake herself up a little.

"Are you okay?" The voice of Matthew Wilkins asked, as she realised she must have drifted out of focus again. "Annie, are you okay?"

"Shit, I'm sorry, I didn't mean to fall asleep. *Did* I fall asleep?" Annie asked, looking down at the teacher, with his scruffy dark hair and blue eyes, standing within a few feet of her. Until then, she had been fairly sure he probably had no idea what her name even was. "Sorry, I guess I have a lot on my mind, and I haven't been sleeping too well recently, I guess."

"Anything serious I can help you with?" He asked her, his scruffy hair falling across one of those blue eyes. "I'm not an ogre, you know. I was young once, I can understand the trials and tribulations of college."

"I get that, Mr. Wilkins, really, cause you're like, only a couple years older than me, but really, it's nothing important. I promise, I'll try and concentrate harder in the future." She assured him, feeling the color rising up her face.

"Well, I'm glad you realise that I'm human, and I hope you will talk to me if you ever need an impartial ear. Now, I need to set up for my next class. I hope you'll excuse me." He smiled, then started back down the auditorium steps to the podium where he taught from, rubbing the previous lesson from the chalkboard. Annie gathered her things, and made her way out.

Once outside, she started to make her way toward the frat house where her twin brother, André, lived. Instantly, he could tell that there was something wrong with her. Not that she would tell him, but she was starting to get scared now. The dreams had always changed before, but now they were all the same, or at least the last few had been. Before the dreams had progressed naturally, night by night, through the lives that they portrayed, the same lives that had lived within the dreams for so long, lives which had paralleled her own since the very first had occurred so many years earlier. The worst part was, that the dreams revolved around *her*, and all the friends she had picked up along the way.

At 7pm, Annie left the frat house, and made her way back to the dorm room she shared with a girl named Joanna. When she got there, Joanna was watching TV with her boyfriend, Curt. They didn't notice Annie as she entered the communal living area, and went into the room that they shared. Her bed was next to the window, which looked over the playing fields, where most of the guys played football in the evenings. She sat and looked out at the last few who were holding on until the light was completely gone. A short way further was the narrow river, and the rather overly grand bridge that crossed it. Every evening, Annie would watch for Matthew Wilkins as he made his way across the bridge, and around the fields to the dorm house for his meeting with his faculty advisor, Jerry Hathaway.

Ever since he had arrived to teach anthropology at the college, Matthew Wilkins had received his fair share of admiring female fans. Annie was probably the quietist of all of them. She had never been the type to shout about her feelings, although she did suspect that several people might have guessed the truth. He was a good-looking man. The scruffy hair was long enough to reach his shoulders, and the blue of his eyes was piercing, looking right into the very core of who - or what - ever he was looking at any given moment. From the very first moment she had seen him, from the back in an overcrowded room, she had felt a pull towards him that she could no sooner explain to her self than to anyone else. He was no more than a couple of years older than her, nearing his final exams. She smiled at the thought of him. He was handsome, and charming, *and* he knew her name. He was interesting, too, unlike many of the other teachers who were bogged down by facts and figures. But that was beside the point. He was young enough to be obtainable, and a lot of the girls had set their sights on him for that very reason.

That evening, Joanna and Curt went out, while Annie sat alone in the dorm room, reading a textbook on ancient cultures. Egyptian pyramids, Mayan temples, the mythical land of Atlantis, the ancient Romans, Greeks, even the Vikings of Norse legend. As she leafed through the pages, she knew already that the land of her dreams was not featured within them, because she was pretty sure by now that the land of her dreams was limited to them, and did not exist within the real world. The land where her dreams took place seemed to be only a small part of a larger civilisation, one that had many people, in cities much the same as that one. The worst part was that it felt so real. She felt like with every dream she was becoming more a part of the community within them. The fact that it felt so real, but that she was unable to find any evidence of its existence, scared her immensely.

She had to get out, she realised. The room was warm and damp, the promise of rain left unfulfilled. There was only one place to go on a weeknight when she couldn't sleep, and had a need for faceless company. She locked the dorm room door, and started to make her way across campus toward the college coffee house.

It was the same as every other college coffee house she had ever seen on TV, with mismatched furniture, under used lighting, and poetry students all trying desperately to grow a little facial hair on their over academic chins, which they would trim into little wisps of fluff. Annie loved it in there. She always ordered a hot chocolate, which she topped with cinnamon, and sat in an armchair that looked out toward the little stage area where the fluffy chinned students recited their poetry, hoping beyond all hope that this would be the night a publisher would be out to find them. She listened to them without much interest, because she really was too pre-occupied to care about terribly much other than her own situation. She was just about to order her second hot chocolate when Matthew Wilkins sat down on the sofa across from her.

"Ready to talk yet?" He asked, a gentle smile on his face.

"Not really, Mr. Wilkins." Annie replied.

"We're not in class now, Annie. Call me Matthew, I hate being called Mr. Wilkins, it makes me feel like I'm 60, or my dad." He told her, the smile spreading slightly further.

"Alright, not really, Matthew."

"I don't mind if it's something really silly. I said earlier that I was willing to listen, so please, talk to me, tell me what's on your mind." He persisted. Annie pressed her eyes closed, trying to decide just how much she was able to tell this man who should be such a stranger, but whom she already knew better than people she had known far longer.

"You'll think I'm crazy, and I'm not sure I'm ready for the faculty to think I'm crazy quite yet."

"Ah! But as I said, right now, I'm just regular old Matthew, and not a teacher, so please, talk to me. I promise I won't think you're crazy unless you really are, in which case, I'll call the psych department and have them come do a case study on you. It will probably make the academic papers, and then all the colleges in the country will know just how crazy you are. But then again, I might just keep the truth to myself, because I really am a rather friendly guy when I want to be." He was still smiling, more and more by the moment. Annie rolled her eyes, and rubbed her forehead with the back of her hand.

"Fine, but the moment you start to look for a phone to call the funny farm, I'm shutting up!" She finally smiled herself. Now though, she wasn't sure where to start with trying to explain things to him. She decided to start with the most recent dreams. "Well, I've been dreaming about this girl, trapped in a room, and it is so dark. There are these little holes near the top of the walls of the room, but they aren't letting in any light, so I'm assuming that it must be nighttime. There are noises outside the room, people talking to me in hushed voices. I've come to the conclusion that the girl in the dream is me, although I've never seen my face. Then, all of a sudden, I'm outside, and it's daytime, and everyone is treating me like I've done something seriously wrong. They just don't realise that everything is coming to an end, that our little civilisation is going to have to cut and run much sooner than they think, because they don't want to believe that the quake is coming. And I'll be shutting up now because you're looking at me as if I really *am* mad."

"How long have you been having these dreams?"

He asked her, his brow furrowed.

"Longer than I can remember, but before they've been different every time. I've had this same one about the isolation chamber for the past few nights. It's a little concerning, because I don't like the idea that they aren't progressing any more. They've become real to me now." She shook her head, and glanced at her watch. "Look at the time! I've got a morning lecture, first thing, and I've taken up all this time talking. I'd better get back and get some sleep. Thanks for listening."

"No problem, I said I was here to help. Actually, I'd like to talk some more with you, maybe record the conversation, if you weren't opposed to that."

"Why? You really think I'm fruit loops, don't you!" She looked at him doubtfully.

"No! Come on, I'll walk you back to the dorm house, and we can set up a meeting. I swear I don't think you're crazy. I know too much about the dreaming consciousness to ever think anyone mad for them. Come on, it really is starting to get late, even the bum fluff crew have dispersed." He grinned at her. Despite her miss giving's, she found herself smiling back, and they walked together out into the night air.

It was a warm night for the time of year. Early spring usually meant showers, and chilly winds, but it had been fairly mild that week, and the students had all taken to discarding jackets and sweaters in anticipation of warmer weather to come. Annie knew that there could still be cold weather in store, so hadn't been quite so rash yet, but even she had opted for a thinner sweater than she normally would.

They walked along, chatting about this and that. Matthew told her some things about the place where he had grown up, down in New Mexico, a short way from an Indian reservation, where his father had helped as a medical doctor. Every now and then, she had to remind herself that they actually were both there, walking side by side, knowing that half the female students, and several of the males, would be jealous at the mere prospect of some one as mundane as Annie with the hot property that was Matthew Wilkins.

When they finally reached the door to Annie's dorm room, they had set up a meeting for that Saturday, at his apartment. He gave her his address, and walked away with a promise to see her in classes. As she went into her room, undressed, and climbed into bed, she did so with the knowledge that she now had an ear in which to pour all of her secret awareness.

Chapter Two

I could not see a thing. One night in the isolation chamber was my punishment, one that I had no choice but to endure. It was not my fault, though. They did not give me a chance to explain, Alexis did not give me a chance to explain. My shoulder hurt from when Brace threw me, and I found it hard to move. I do not think it was my fault that Malarchy and I were growing closer than we should, nor indeed was it his. It had been happening for a long while, since at least three sun cycles before. I understood that Alexis did not like the fact, for she had once tried to ensnare Malarchy, even though she knew her destiny lay with Brace.

Through the ventilation holes around the top of the room, I could see the stars. It had been dark for a long time now. From the position of the stars, I could tell that the sun would rise soon, and that my punishment would soon be over, even if that meant that I would have to face my parents, and the displeasure that they would have at the thought of me wanting to join with anyone other than Haltar. They knew that I would never be happy with him, and yet they still insisted that it would one day come to be.

I had heard tales before of people who had spent too long in the isolation chamber, and went insane when they were released. They would have to execute them when that happened, like Brace's cousin, from Isis. He was in the chamber for three moon cycles before they let him out. He was insane, and they had to take him into the trees to be executed. Brace enjoyed telling us of his cousin when there was little else to do.

Being alone gives you time to think. I could remember a long time before, when I was younger, many years earlier, when the boats set out. There were many of them, sent to find us the new lands that we knew we would someday need. Some went one way, while the others went another way, and they found the land that they had sought. When they came back, they spoke of the wonderful coloured men that they had met, that talked and acted differently from us. Our elders even tried to take influences from their cultures. My brother, Alim, had wanted to go with them, but our young age at the time meant that we were not permitted to do so. He was impatient, but I knew that we would be going to those lands soon enough, that when the quakes came, we would have no choice but to make the journeys to the new lands, out across the oceans to these civilisations which we hoped would welcome us into their worlds.

"Anicia?" I heard a voice call to me. It was the

voice of Malarchy, who was taking great risk to speak with me.

"Malarchy, I am here, but you should not be, my love. I will see you soon enough, please go before they capture you here. They would punish you much further than the isolation chamber." I called back to him, in little more than a whispered voice.

"I will see you in the trees, when the sun is up. Come to me, please. I need you near to me, Anicia." He told me. I could feel warm tears within my eyes, knowing that he would risk all for me to come to him.

"I will come. Now, please go before you are seen, my love."

He did not respond, but I could hear him still breathing outside for a moment, before the sound of his footsteps carried him away from me. He would be returning to his home temple for the rest of the night, what little may remain of it, for the sky was now starting to lighten a little, and I was aware that the sun would rise soon.

When morning finally came, I was released from the isolation chamber. Alim was waiting for me in the gardens. We were always so close, sharing the same life bond, having entered the world on the same day. Now, as I met Alim in the gardens, he spoke softly but quickly.

"Haltar heard of what happened last night. He is angry, Anicia." Alim told me.

"Haltar can go to hell, as far as I am concerned, and Alexis may join him. There is little I can say in my own defence, but I would hope that you, my brother, may understand that I am not dedicated to Haltar." I spat at him. Alim did not look impressed at my words.

"Anicia, you do not have a choice. You are

promised to Haltar, you are his whether or not you like the situation. You *will* continue the lifeline with Haltar. It is destined for you, as the daughter of our emperor to marry the son of the High Priest, just as I must marry Kylin, the daughter of the High Priest. We have no choice, it was decided before our births." Alim told me. I knew he spoke the truth, but I was not willing to quickly accept what he was telling me. "And I *do* understand, Anicia, for I trust Malarchy more than many, more even than Haltar, but it does not change the situation."

"How can it be fair that I will have to be faithful to Haltar forever, when he may have any woman he chooses. Why can I not have Malarchy?" I cried, looking at my brother, who looked back at me with disapproval. "I know the answer, Alim, I do not need you to supply me with it. Come, Grey is waiting for us."

We made our way to the temple of the well, where Alim's friend Grey was waiting for us. The temple was empty apart from Grey, and we were able to talk there freely.

"How was your night in the chamber?" Grey asked me. I sometimes wondered whether my brother's friend was actually more *my* friend.

"As it should have been, I would suppose. Thank you for asking, Grey." I replied, as we took seats around the temple.

"Grey, you understand more about the lifeline than I do. Please, would you explain it to Anicia, for she seems to fail to grasp the details of the need for it." Alim requested.

"There is no way out of the lifebond, Anicia." Grey told me gently. "When we are born, the charts are plotted to make the best matches for us. The lifebond is settled then, and is eternally binding for females. The lifebond is put in place so that the lifeline will continue in the most prosperous ways, with the most important families becoming interlinked. I know that it is unfair that you will never be allowed to fulfil your bond with Malarchy, but the date for the joining between you and Haltar is set. There is no escape from it. The only thing that could separate you would be the great quake, But Niall predicted that the quake is still at least a sun cycle away from now."

"I will never love Haltar." I told them defiantly.

"That is not the point of the lifebond. The point is the continuation of the lifeline, and that has very little to do with love. Alim is one of our few exceptions. I am not even lucky enough to have a lifebond to enter into. There is no better thing than to have the future foreseen for us, Anicia, and you should feel blessed to know what lies ahead for you." Grey sighed, and I knew of what he spoke, for his was truly a forbidden love.

"Why can you not just be happy that you will be bound to Haltar within the next few moon cycles, as I will be with Kylin?" Alim questioned.

"Because Haltar is spiteful, malicious. He has no concept of kindness. When I see him, all I know is that I will never love him, and I do not wish to spend the rest of my days bound to him. I will never be bound to Haltar."

"You have no choice, sister. Now, it may be best if you returned to the home temple for the day. I think it would do you well to consider your future for longer than just last night. Grey will walk with you." Alim commanded. Grey nodded his head, knowing that Alim's request was his command.

We left the temple of the well, and started in the

direction of the home temple. As we started past the trees, Grey turned to me, with a smile. "Go to Malarchy, I know he waits for you within the trees. If Alim finds out, he will probably have me thrown into isolation, but your happiness is more important to me than anything. And for what it is worth, I understand that Haltar is not the correct match for you. I will cover for you if I have to, but in the meantime, I may go to Alina, if that is alright."

"Thank you, Grey." I smiled, and went into the trees. I already knew where I would find Malarchy. He would be gathering leaves for his father's needs, as our medicine man. And there he stood, pulling leaves from the trees, which his father would use to wrap wounds, and to make elixirs to help heal. His dark hair reached his shoulders now, shining where the sun hit it. His strong, beautiful shoulders were darkened from the sun. "Malarchy."

"Do any know that you are here?" He asked me, his face smiling.

"Only Grey, but he will not give us away, for he is with my hand maiden at the home temple. We are alone here, Malarchy." I replied, moving to him, his outstretched arms pulling me towards him. He touched my face with his hand, and I kissed him where his life could be felt at his wrist. "Alim says that I am hopeless. He tells me that there is no way out of the lifebond, that I must learn to love Haltar."

"That is the truth, you must be bonded to Haltar. You will learn to love him, eventually. But believe me, he will never love you as much as I, and I shall never love another. I think I may be lucky that I will never have to be bound to anyone, because I will never have to force myself into loving anyone other than you. If there were options for you, then there would be no problem." He smiled, pressing his lips to mine, holding me tightly within his arms.

"I will never love him as much as I love you." I whispered. Together, we stood in the sun, but it was love that warmed my heart.

Chapter Three

Annie felt uncomfortable as she knocked on the door to Matthew Wilkins' apartment. He opened it quickly, still buttoning his shirt over his smooth, tanned chest.

"Hey, Annie, come on in. Make yourself comfortable; I'll be with you in a minute. Sorry about the smoke, I burnt breakfast." Matthew greeted. She entered the small two-room apartment, and looked around. There was a small kitchen area with a stove and sink. There was an overstuffed orange couch, and a couple of green easy chairs. A coffee table that looked as if it had been made in shop class stood between the chairs in the centre of the room. There was a doorway without a door, beyond which there was a bedroom, with a double bed. A dream catcher hung from the doorframe. In one corner of the living room was an old black and white TV, which was tuned into a local news station. On top of the TV, there was a framed photograph of Matthew Wilkins in graduation robes, standing next to an older man, who Annie figured must be Matthew's father. In the other corner, there was a rather large desk, with a computer and a great deal of papers on. It was the sort of place that she could see would not be inhabited by Matthew Wilkins for very long.

She sat gingerly on the edge of the couch, and felt herself sinking slightly. Adjusting her position, she found a spot that didn't seem quite so bottomless. Matthew was in the kitchen, boiling the kettle, and chewing on a piece of blackened toast. He opened a cupboard, and took out a couple of cups.

"Tea or coffee?" He called to her.

"Tea, thanks." Annie replied. A few minutes later, he brought two cups of black tea, milk, and sugar into the living room area. He set it down on the coffee table, next to a small tape recorder. He offered her milk and sugar, but she declined.

"Is it okay if I record this?" Matthew asked, adding two sugars to his own cup.

"Sure, it's fine, although I'm not sure that it'll be a hit!" She smiled. "How long have you been here, Mr. Wilkins?"

"Since last August. I transferred from out of state. And it's Matthew, remember." He replied. Annie sipped at the hot cup in her hand, and wondered what she was supposed to say next. She'd never been alone with a male before, at least not *that* alone with a male before, and she wasn't really sure how she was expected to act in the situation. He took the decision out of her hands. "Where do you come from?"

"Right here. Well, obviously not *right* here, but I grew up in a duplex about fifteen miles from here. My brother André and I decided early on that we would stay close, after my father died when we were kids. We didn't want to move too far away from mom." Annie explained. Matthew, who had taken a place on one of the green easy chairs, listened, looking sympathetic. "Sorry, you didn't want my life history, did you? We should probably get on before the whole morning is gone."

"That's okay. I really just want you to tell me about your dreams, what you think they mean. What I think really isn't important at the moment." He said, picking up the tape recorder, and pressing the record button. "Go for it, Annie."

"Well," Annie started, putting her cup back on the coffee table. Now that she was sitting there with him, she wasn't really sure what she was supposed to be telling him, so she decided to start with a description of the land within her dreams. "The land is lush and green, and there are trees all around the settlement where I live. It's called Aqui Milam, the settlement. Strange that I should know that, because I know very little else. There is more to our civilisation. I know that there is a place where people build boats, which they hope will be our salvation when the quake comes, which it will do soon. There are amazing rivers, which circle the land on which we live. Aqui Milam is at the very heart of the continent, I don't know why I refer to it as such, because it isn't that large, but it seems more vital than an island would do. I'm sorry, that sounds a little confusing, doesn't it? I don't know how else to explain it though. It's very warm, but not heavily hot like it can be here sometimes. Oh, and the water tastes so amazing, like really expensive bottled water, and we get it from the temple of the well.

"There are these buildings, not many of them. One of them seems to be the home for nearly everyone in the settlement, except for the medicine man and the High Priest's family, and it's huge. In the other settlements, there are small dwellings, but we are at the centre of the civilisation, so we all live in that one, large temple. I'm the child of an emperor, that much I am sure of, my brother and I. The temple reminds me more of the Mayan temples, but there is an element of the Egyptian pyramids thrown in for fair measure. I'll draw them for you later if you like.

"I don't have very many friends, to be honest. I have my brother's friend, who is very good to me, and my handmaiden. There are others, including one girl who I sense does not like me at all, and who reminds me greatly of someone I know. I won't implicate anyone in case this gets into anyone's hands. My brother knows everyone - my dream brother that is. He knows loads of the people who went on the journeys of discovery when we were younger. They have found us places to go after Niall's quake comes. I have no idea how I know some names and not others, and how some facts are so crystalline to me.

"Then there's him. Another one whose name I don't know. He and I have gotten closer and closer over the past few years. That's how I ended up in the isolation chamber, because I'm really not allowed to get close to him. As far as I can tell, I'm supposed to marry this other guy, who reminds me of an ogre, the proper kind. The problem is, I think I love the guy I'm not supposed to even talk to. He has been the same person all along, well, they all have. We've all grown up together. He is as familiar to me as if I really *do* know him. I've managed to find most of the other people in my dreams, like Gary Hutchins, and my good friend Barry. I said I wouldn't implicate anyone, didn't I? Oh, well, done now. I didn't meet them until a long time after they first turned up in my dreams, but they haven't changed, they've always looked the same. Does that make sense?" Annie finished. Matthew nodded, and Annie sighed with relief. She wasn't sure exactly whether he believed her though, after all, it was a little far fetched that all the people in her real life had been in her dreams *before* she even met them.

"So, what do you think they mean?" He asked her, looking at her intently, those blue eyes of his searching her core for the answers she held.

"I think it's all been a waste of your time, me coming here, and I'll leave you to your Saturday, if you don't mind too much." Annie replied, wondering how quickly she could make her exit if she ran.

"I think you're wrong. I told you how I had grown up near an Indian reservation, well, during that time I learned a great deal about reincarnation. They believed strongly in past lives, and that the soul is constantly recycled. Other religious beliefs take the same view, by the way - I'll be covering that next semester. Anyway, getting back to the point, the fact that you managed to find people from your dreams within this life, may just mean that you are dreaming of your past existence. I can see the doubt in your eyes, and I'm guessing that this is when you start looking for a funny farm for me, because the next thing I'm going to suggest is that you allow me to have you hypnotically regressed." Matthew told her. It wasn't the answer she had been expecting. In fact, she had had little doubt that he would not believe her at all.

"You want to hypnotise me so that I remember stuff I did a hundred years ago?" She asked, doubtfully.

"My guess would be a few thousand years or so, and it wouldn't be me hypnotising you, but yes. I have a friend who's a doctor. He specialises in regressions, and I think he would really be able to help you. The fact is, these dreams of yours are probably keeping you from leading your normal life, so if you were able to find out what they meant, you may just be able to get on with the real world more easily." He smiled at her, and for a moment, she felt at ease. She rested her hand across her eyes for a moment, contemplating the thought. There were many reasons she could think of why she shouldn't do it, but there were better reasons *for* doing it. Finally, she let her hand drop.

"Okay." She agreed finally, instantly having second thoughts, but prepared to commit to it.

"Good, I'll call the doctor and set it up. I'll let you know the dates on Monday after class. It's probably best if you don't tell too many people, because even though I don't think you're mad, doesn't mean others won't."

"I wouldn't worry too much about that. Other than me, you're the only one who knows about my dreams. Not even André knows."

"Why's that, do you think?" He asked her.

"Because in my dreams, I have this brother, and I don't know whether my real brother would accept that. I mean, my dream brother *is* my real brother, so I shouldn't really be that worried, it's just that I don't think he'd understand is all. I love André, I really do, but he has no idea that the rest of the world isn't about him. I think that this might all be a bit too much for him to handle." Annie replied, looking back into his blue eyes.

"But there are other people in your dreams that represent people in your life, surely he would understand that much."

"Doubtful, Matthew, I've known him for far too long. And now, I really should get going. I've taken all your morning, again with the time stealing. Mind you, if all these people in my dreams are people that I am destined to know, then who *is* this guy that I'm getting close to, the one I'm not supposed to talk to?"

"The only thing I can think is that he would be your soul mate, the one other soul that yours will always search for. You would be lucky to find him, because few of us ever do."

Annie stood and made her way to the door. Matthew was within steps behind her, and held the door open as she walked out. The hallway was flooded with afternoon light, pouring in through the open window at the top of the stairwell.

"Well, if we're going to be soul mates, I guess we'd better meet soon." She smiled as she stepped out into the hallway.

"You never know, you may have already met. Stranger things have happened before than that. Bear in mind that sometimes the soul takes a different form to the one that you have known before." He told her. "Anyway, I'll see you on Monday. Until then, sleep well."

He closed the door behind her, and she made her way toward the stairwell. She paused for a moment, breathing in the air that smelt of spring. She thought for a moment she might have completely lost her senses at some point during the morning. She wasn't sure she would ever be able to tell Matthew Wilkins that she had already met the man who was her soul mate.

Chapter Four

He couldn't help it, she was perfect. Of course, he was never going to be able to tell her that she was. The moment he had spotted Annie Bouvais at the back of his over crowded auditorium, Matthew had realised that she was absolutely perfect. It wasn't just the way she looked, although her dark hair and green eyes were very nice. It was more the feeling of electricity he could feel every time he caught her looking directly at him. She usually averted her eyes fairly quickly when they met his, but he could feel them looking at him sometimes. She was tall and fine, but not so thin that there was nothing there, and everything about her was, in his opinion, perfection.

He had thought she might think him crazy for his idea about the regression, but she seemed to accept it fairly quickly. That pleased him. The doctor would be happy to help, and it was sure to mean that they would have to spend some time together outside of class times. And she had opened up to him, told him about her dreams. Surely that must prove that she was able to talk to him about anything. He suspected that this may be grasping at straws, but if those were all he *could* grasp at, he would take them.

It had been no accident that breakfast got the chance to burn that morning. He had been busy watching for her through the telescope in his bedroom. It wasn't the first time he had watched for her. The first time, he had managed to burn breakfast so badly that his whole apartment complex had been evacuated. He had timed the buttoning of his shirt to perfection, fastening all but the top two buttons as he opened the door, allowing her a quick glimpse of his smooth chest.

Now, he crossed the space between the door and his telescope quickly, knowing that she would be walking out into the afternoon sun any moment. It did not take long for her to get outside, and he watched her as she made her way back to the dorm house where she lived. It was too far away for him to see by the naked eye, even though he could spot her a mile away. The way she walked was fantastic, with just the hint of a dance that only she knew, and that he was sure only he noticed. He watched her until she reached the dorm house, and then adjusted the telescope back to Annie's dorm window (which he had located within a few days of first spotting her in the back of his class). After he realised that she slept next to the window, he had watched her sleeping whenever the nerve allowed him. He returned to the living room and crossed to the telephone. He lifted the receiver of the old phone, and dialled the familiar number quickly. It rang four and a half times before there was an answer.

"Hello?" The voice of Matthew's childhood friend, Brandon, called down the line to him.

"Hey, Brandon, buddy, it's me." He called back, smiling to himself.

"Mattie! To what do I owe this rather rare pleasure, man?" Asked his friend.

"I need a regression done for a girl in one of my classes. Is the doc still in the business?" Matthew asked, instantly regretting the fact that he had said the word 'girl', because Brandon was probably now going to pounce on the least important fact in the sentence.

"Girl, hey?" Brandon laughed.

"How did I know you'd pick that fact out of all of them? She's one of my students, and that would be unethical, wouldn't it! Besides that, I'm trying to be the good guy these days, and as far as I can recall, I never had anywhere near as much talent as you did with the girls. Now, is your dad at home, or should I call back?"

"No, he's out with your dad, attending a sing for someone or other. I'll get him to call you when he gets back. You know, I don't mean to tease you, bud. So, is she hot or what?"

"Well, I'll put it this way. If she weren't my student, I can't see me saying no, but then, you know my type, Bran, so I'm not sure what that says about her."

"It says enough! Bring her down, I'm sure dad would be willing to help out. And don't be a stranger, man; we miss you around here, you know. We're missing one for basket ball still."

"I'll be down for summer break in a couple months, anyway. It's good to talk to you, buddy. And if you could ask your dad to call me, I'd appreciate that, Bran."

"Later, buddy."

As Matthew hung up the phone, he had to smile to himself. Brandon had been his best friend since they were four years old, and their fathers had been involved in the medical conflicts that had been occurring on the reservation. Brandon's father had been working as a psychiatrist for a long while, using his hypnotic techniques to help give insights into deeper problems. Matthew's father was a medical doctor, though, and his methods were seen as going against the natural order of things. Brandon's father had been helpful in getting him accepted into their communities. That summer, Brandon and Matthew had become fast friends. Matthew had been a small child, a little sickly at times, until that summer. The move to the small town, a stones throw from the reservation, had improved his health no end. He and Brandon had spent so much time playing basketball outside of Matthew's house that within weeks, he was stronger than anyone would have thought possible. He became a strong, fine young man, and while his friend grew up to be a bit of a jock, Matthew was no athlete, but was definitely the one that people aspired to be.

At school, when he was a sophomore, Matthew had attracted the eyes of almost half the girls in his class. Brandon had been the one that had gone after them, though. It wasn't that he was particularly shy, or that he was afraid of girls, but he just found himself ignoring the advances of them all. He had tried dating, of course, but he had never gotten in further than a few dates before things ended. In time, he came to realise that he was not supposed to merely date girl after girl, he was supposed to be waiting for one in particular. Spotting Annie Bouvais, he knew that he had been right that day, a few years earlier, when he had decided that there would only ever be one girl for him.

Now he realised that she was looking for a soul mate. It wasn't fair, because he had waited all this time, only to have her stolen from him like that. He jumped up from his seat, and started to pace around the small room, shaking his head, feeling his hair around his shoulders. His mother would tell him it was far too long, and he supposed that it may well be, but he wasn't about to hack it all off at that moment. Besides, he had always hoped that the long hair might keep the girls away, but he had started to realise that it sometimes got the opposite reaction. His worry initially was that Annie would find it repulsive, but she hadn't seemed to mind too much.

He had to get some air, he decided. His best option was going to the local market. The burnt toast that had made up his breakfast had been the last food in the house, so he needed to get some supplies, anyway. He grabbed his car keys from a dish on his desk, and made his way out of the apartment. There was a parking lot under the building, and Matthew's old, white Corvette convertible was parked in his spot as always. When Matthew was a boy, the car had been his grandfather's, but when his grandfather passed away a few years earlier, the car had been left to him. It was a large car, with bench seats and white wall tyres, and it was perfection as far as he was concerned. The engine rumbled as he drove out of the lot, and to the store, a ten-minute ride off campus.

At the market, he pushed his little cart around, gathering the essential items he thought he might need for a week worth of meals. He didn't really like having to cook for himself, although he could. He just found that the effort was more than he could really be bothered with. Cooking and cleaning for one was not his idea of what life was meant to be like. He had rather imagined that by the time he reached his twenties (not that he was far in to them) that he would be well and truly settled, and that he would have someone else around to share the fun with. Now, though, he was resigned to the fact that he was going to live on frozen fish sticks and instant Jell-O. Of course, he made sure he picked up all the important items - bread, milk, eggs. Ice cream flavours were his for the picking, but he stuck to chocolate, guessing that he was really far too safe at heart. He did, however, pick up three different types of sprinkles. He was just working his way to fruit and vegetables when Ali Rice appeared round a corner.

Ali was in the same class as Annie, and he got the feeling that she was the one Annie had been referring to when she mentioned the other girl from her dreams, the girl she didn't like. She was like a shark, constantly working her way through the waters, trying to get her teeth into anyone and anything she thought might belong to someone else. He knew that she was dating a guy named Barry, but had a theory that she was out to try and get him. During his first month of teaching, she had been spotted wearing her hair in at least four different colors (it was naturally blond, but not in a good way), and had made an effort to flirt loudly with a couple of guys who were sitting either side of her in the front row every time he passed her. If she'd really wanted to figure out what he was looking for in a girl, all he had to do was to look at Annie, because she was all he wanted, all he could imagine he would ever need in a girl, even if there was no way in the world he was going to get her. Now here Ali was, yet again, heading his way for another attempt on his manhood.

"Hello, Mr. Wilkins." She smiled rather overly sweetly. There was no escape now.

"Ms Rice." He smiled back, forcing his lips to turn upwards at the girl. She was far too thin, with rather bad breast implants and far too much make-up. He couldn't help but dislike her.

"Nice mix of food groups, Mr. Wilkins." She smiled again, peering into his cart at the frozen fish sticks with disdain.

"Ah, well, my sister and her kid are coming up to stay for a few days, so I figured I should stock up on kid foods in case he's a fussy eater." Matthew lied. He was an only child, and so the likelihood of him having a sister, or of her having a child, was fairly non-existent.

"Well, you don't have any cookies or candy in there." Ali smiled yet again, in what looked like her best 'I'm really very shy, but I want you for my own' smile. He wasn't convinced by it for even the slightest of moments.

"Very good point, thanks Ms Rice. See you in class on Monday." He said, and walked away quickly. He grabbed a couple cans of beans, some rice, and chilli in a jar. A frozen pizza was a last minute choice. He paid for the items he was purchasing, and piled them into paper sacks. As he put them in the Corvette, he realised that he had left his change behind. But he wasn't going back now. He had just spotted Annie, and couldn't stand the thought of walking that close to her again so soon. After all, it had taken all of his concentration to cope with her being in his apartment that morning. Then he realised she was not alone. Gary Hutchins was sitting next to her on the wall, and they were acting rather too friendly for friends. As he got into the car, and started the engine loudly, he felt a little like crying.

Chapter Five

Eventually, Malarchy had to let go of me. I sat watching him, his strong shoulders reaching high into the trees. He hummed as he worked, the sweet melody that I had given to him when we were younger, and our meetings were not forbidden. I sang along with his humming, and soon we had a harmony in place of the melody. But all too soon, our sweet harmony was interrupted by the quickened voice of Grey, telling us that we had to return to the home temple immediately. The elders had called an important meeting, and we were all expected to be there. We hurried toward the home temple together, but I was aware that if we were to arrive together, then there would be questions over where we had been.

"Wait, Grey, we cannot go in together." I told my friend. "Remember that you have been with Alina while you should have been with me."

"She is right." Malarchy agreed, stopping and holding his hand out to me. "Don't worry, I will wait until you have been inside. I am not really required to be there as you are."

"Thank you, Malarchy." Grey acknowledged him. I took Malarchy's hand, and rose to him for a kiss before parting. He made his way back into the trees, and Grey and I continued.

"Grey, I know that you will answer me truthfully. If I ask you a question, you will give me no lies. I am troubled by certain thoughts that have been coming to me recently. May I speak with you freely, friend?" I asked him.

"You may speak of everything except for your love for Malarchy. That would put you in as much difficulty as if I spoke to you of my day with Alina. Ask me your questions, Anicia, and I will answer them with as much truth as I can." Grey answered me.

"Well, I am worried. I am feeling that we, as a culture, are growing unstable. I do not know how I feel it, only that I do. I feel that we will not make it through this sun cycle before the great quake comes." I told him in concern.

"Why do you feel this?"

"Last night, in the isolation chamber, I could feel the ground. It was strange, unsettled. I think that the great quake that Niall predicted is going to come sooner than we thought." I told him.

"That may be so. My brother Blue, who lives in Isis, he says that the bay feels to be getting smaller now than ever, that the land seems to be dropping to meet the waters."

"Then do you feel that it may be so?"

"Yes, Anicia, I do. I think that this may be why the meeting has been called. The elders are starting to realise that we do not have as much time as they thought we did. Others may not be willing to listen to these thoughts, but the truth is, I think we may have to leave Aqui Milam before the next sun cycle begins."

"Will they be ready for the move from here?" I asked, knowing in truth that we may not.

"They have been building ships in Isis and Fenda for a long time now. Niall's quake will last for seven days, or so he predicted. It will be followed by a great fire which will burn the ground until no thing remains, before the lands fall into the waters forever. If we do not leave soon enough, then the waters will swallow us as it takes the land. There will be space for most on the ships, although I am willing to guess that some may be left. We will make it to the new lands, as the people of Aqui Milam, because we are, or rather you are, the children of those in power. It will be hard for you, as your parents will go to the West. You, along with Alim, will go to the East, with the children of medicine and healing. There will be the people who seek to make the world better through caring for others." Grey replied.

"Then Malarchy will come to the East, with me?"

"Yes. The children of religion on the other hand will go to the West, which you may assume will include Haltar. The only thing that will make a difference to that matter is if you are by then bound to Haltar, because then you will have to go to the West with him. I rather have to hope that that will not happen, as I would rather miss you if we were parted."

"Then is it wise for me to hope that the quake will

come before I am bound to Haltar?"

"Please, do hope, for I would rather hope that in our new civilisation, I would not be forbidden from seeing Alina."

"You are filling her mind with non-sense, again friend." Alim's voice called to us as we reached the home temple. He was angry again. "Come, we must hurry, Anicia. Our father is expecting us at his side. And do not hope, Grey, that any other civilisation will accept that you want to be one with a hand maiden,"

"You are cruel, Alim. I hope that time will soften your disposition." I told my brother, but allowed him to lead me to the chamber where our father was already holding his meeting.

The room was filled with people that I did not know, but whom I realised must have come from Isis, Fenda, other places where they were concerned with the quake that was due to come. Our father was speaking his words; everyone else listened restlessly to them.

"But Niall said that the quake would not hit here for another sun cycle. Do you mean to tell us that the quake is to come sooner?" A man asked.

"We must start to accept that the waters are rising, and that this may be an indication that our land is sinking in preparation for the quake to come upon us. We may not have another sun cycle in which to prepare for our journeys. We need to take action to get the ships built *now*. There is talk that the ground can already be felt to shake at times. We do not have time to debate the facts any further. Anyone in Isis or Fenda who are not already working on the ships will be from this moment on. In the other towns, you will be expected to start gathering supplies for the journeys. There is no more time now, so this meeting is adjourned for this night."

The room emptied quickly, leaving Alim and I alone with our father, He looked on us, his children, as if we were merely two more of his people.

"Father, we will be of this service also." Alim assured our father, who looked at him as if seeing him for the first time in many moon cycles.

"No, Alim, your position means that you are not required to help with these trivialities. However, it may be necessary to move your joinings to sooner than was planned. Haltar and Kylin are aware of this. You will be joined in two moon cycles from now." Our father told us. At his words, I felt sickened, and my knees started to feel that they might give way at any moment. If I was to be joined to Haltar so soon, then I would not be free from him ever.

"If you think that best, Father." Alim told him. Within my own heart, I was unable to accept that it would be so.

"Alim, your joining will take place first, and Anicia will be joined half a moon cycle later." He told us, and for a moment, I felt relief, that there was a chance that I may be saved. I tried to keep my face from revealing my thoughts to my father. "Now, adjourn to sleeping chambers, please."

Alim turned from my father, and started to his sleeping chamber which was located at the other end of the home temple, while I turned to the direction of my own. I was met there by Alina, who made ready my things for the night ahead.

"He does not even look at me, now. He is disappointed that I was with Malarchy, and still he insists that the joinings will take place soon." I told Alina, as I made ready for sleep.

"Grey says that you should be with Malarchy. Grey is wise, and I believe his words." Alina told me in return. "Please, though, do not try to make the joining stop, for I have seen your father when he is displeased, Anicia."

"Do not worry, Alina. Once the quake comes, we will both be free. For now I bid you fair sleep, and dreams of life with Grey." I offered Alina. She bowed to me and left the chamber to go to her own. As I lay on the bed in the centre of the chamber, I hoped for both our sakes that the quake would come as soon as possible.

Chapter Six

Had she seen him as he pulled out of the parking lot? He could have hit himself for reacting like that. She didn't belong to him, after all, so what difference did it make if she was seeing Gary Hutchins? Except that it made him feel sick to think he was going to lose out because of that guy. She had mentioned Gary Hutchins as someone from within her dreams. Was *he* the one, the soul mate that she was looking for? It wasn't fair!

He had pulled away so loudly that half the people in the lot had turned to look at him. His car wasn't exactly inconspicuous, either. He had hoped that he might be able to drive her down to the reservation for the regression in the car. Well, if she hadn't realised who the car belonged to before, she would when he picked her up in it.

He unpacked the groceries, and put them all away, then he started to pace the living room again. If she *had* seen him, she would surely realise that something was wrong with him. Would she realise it was jealousy? How could he have been stupid enough to draw such attention to himself?

"How stupid am I?" He yelled at himself, and started into the bedroom. He trained his telescope back to her room, and focused the lens. He could see her clearly, sitting on the bed, laughing and shaking her head. His heart leapt a little at the sight of her. Then a thought occurred to him. What if she was laughing because of him, and what he had done? She wouldn't do that, though, would she? Not her, not his Annie. She was sweet, pure, special. She wouldn't be so callous, not her.

He watched her for a while longer. There were two guys with her, one of whom he recognised instantly as Gary Hutchins. The other was stocky, with dark hair. He had his arm around her now, and she seemed to be crying, or was she still laughing? If it weren't for the fact that she had been within touching distance so many times recently, he would have ignored the whole thing. But she had been there, that very morning, sitting on the damned orange couch that threatened to swallow people. She had talked openly about her experiences, her thoughts and dreams. She was within his grasp, even if she did seem to run between his fingers like liquid. He would have ignored the way his heart leapt when he saw her if she hadn't been within touching distance so many times within the last few days.

He couldn't stand the thought of her crying. He needed to be near her, make sure that she was all right. But he couldn't just go there without any reason. He tried to think of something that he could use as an excuse for arriving at her door unannounced. After all, if any member of the faculty spotted him, he would have problems. Jerry Hathaway wasn't the only faculty member who lived in the dorm building, and the dean of the university had his offices there as well. If he *did* get spotted, Matthew could have faced dismissal from his position. That may not be such a bad thing, he rationalised, but it did mean he would never see Annie again. That *was* such a bad thing.

As he looked through the telescope again, his stomach knotted a little further. He could go on the pretence that he had managed to arrange something for the regression. But that would be a lie, because he had no more information now than he had when he last saw her. He could take her a book, tell her it was a little extra reading for the course, but then why wasn't he taking the same information to all the other students in his class? All he could really do was watch her from afar, but that didn't seem to be enough for him anymore.

He paced back into the living room, and flopped down onto the orange couch. His elbows started to sink, but he refused to fight it. He was giving up, he decided. She would have to get by without him from now on. She didn't need him, any way. The truth was, she never had. So now he would just let her be alone, and ignore her, pretend she wasn't even there. It didn't take him long to realise that this would be unachievable, and to start laughing at himself rather loudly. He wasn't going to get out of it that easily.

The tape recording machine was still sitting on the coffee table. He rose up, extracting his elbows from the couch, and made a move to pick it up. Pressing first the rewind, then the play buttons, he found the room filled with Annie's voice once more.

"He is as familiar to me as if I really *do* know him. I've managed to find most of the other people in my dreams, like Gary Hutchins, and my good friend Barry. I said I wouldn't implicate anyone, didn't I? Oh, well, done now." Her voice replayed. He smiled at her voice, and realised that when she referred to Gary Hutchins, she did so with a friendly tone, but not an overly affectionate one. Perhaps there was hope after all. He switched the machine off, and as he put it back down, the phone rang loudly.

"Hello?" He called into the receiver as he lifted it to his ear.

"Matthew? It's Doc Harland here. Brandon told me you had a case for me." His friend's father called back to him.

"Hey, Doc, thanks for getting back to me so quickly. It's one of my students. She's been having strange dreams, for *years*. I've interviewed her about them, but it seems like a case for you. There are people in her dreams that she says she met *after* they first appeared in them, lots of people." Matthew smiled at the thought of it all.

"Hmm, sounds interesting. Bring her down here. You know I can't resist a case. How long do you think?" The doctor asked.

"At least a couple thousand years by the sound of things. I'd like to bring her down for a weekend. If we could do the last weekend in April, I'd appreciate it." Matthew requested, hoping that it would be okay for Annie to do that particular set of days.

"I can't see any problems with that. I'll look

forward to seeing you, as I know Brandon will." The doctor agreed. That was only three weeks away, not so very long for him to have to wait, he thought. As he hung up the phone, he realised that he now had an excuse to drive over there and see her.

He didn't take more than a few moments to check he was calm and collected before he grabbed his keys from the counter in the kitchen. He paused long enough to lock the door, before making his way back down to his car. The drive took only a couple of minutes, and before he knew it, he was standing once more in front of her door, his hand raised to rap lightly on the bare wood.

When a mid height blond girl opened the door, he was momentarily confused, hoping that he hadn't chosen the wrong door. The girl looked at him with curiosity, her brown eyes asking who he was without so much as a word.

"You'll be looking for Annie, I guess. Figures, all the cute guys come looking for her. She's entertaining at the moment, but I'll let her know you're here." The girl told him. She gestured for him to follow her into the main communal area that would be shared between the two girls and at least one other. He took a seat, which he didn't sink in to, and watched the girl as she crossed to one of the doors. "Annie, there's someone else to see you."

"Huh?" Annie's voice came from the doorway. She looked around the edge of the door, and gave the slightest of smiles when she saw him. The girl mumbled something that Matthew couldn't make out, and Annie said something in return. The girl giggled a little, then went into the room as Annie came out. "Hi, Mr. Wilkins."

"Hi." He smiled as she came over and sat down on the other couch that rather over filled the area. "Sorry, I didn't mean to disturb you. Your friend said you were entertaining."

"Not really. Joanna thinks she has a sense of humour. How can I help?" She asked, looking at him with those green eyes that he had started to believe were there just for his appreciation.

"Well, I've just spoken to my friend, the doctor. He suggested we go down for the weekend, at the end of the month. It's just under three weeks away, if that's alright with you." He told her, hoping that it would be, because he had already told the doc it would be.

"That sounds perfect, if I can take it that long. I have to admit, the dreams are starting to get to me a little bit. If I could just get past this *one* dream, get to the next day, then I think it would be all right. Sorry, I'm not trying to sound so pathetic, really." She told him. He smiled again.

"It will have to move on eventually, Annie." He tried to assure her. "And it doesn't sound pathetic, either. I'll leave you to your friends."

"Speaking of the devils." She said as the door to her room opened, and two guys came out. He recognised Gary Hutchins straight away. The other one was the stocky guy who'd had his arm around Annie before. Close up, Matthew could see just how green his eyes were. "Gary, André, this is Mr. Wilkins. Actually, Gary, I think you probably already know Mr. Wilkins, right?"

"Sure, Annie, we're in the same class as each other; you know, the one with all the history and culture and stuff. Start paying attention, would you." Gary laughed at her gently, and smiled at him, seeming friendly enough. The other guy didn't look impressed by him, but at least Matthew knew who he was now. "Come on, André, let's get a move on. I could do with a coffee. See you later, Annie."

"Yeah, and make sure you're at the movie theatre by 10. Carlene will shoot me if I don't keep an eye on the two of you." André told his sister. Matthew wasn't sure what that meant, but he assumed that it meant Annie had some sort of date for the evening. Annie walked them over to the door, and pulled it open for them. Again, he could hear them exchange a few words, but couldn't make out what they were. "Nice to meet you!"

"You too." Matthew waved as the two young men left through the door. When Annie turned back to the room, her face was ever so slightly flushed, as if a blush had made its way across her pale complexion.

"Sorry about that. My brother likes to drop by at the weekend. Gary makes things *easier*, because although we're twins, I really don't think we're related sometimes. I swear, André thinks he is above most other people most of the time. I love him and everything, but I wish he'd get off his high horse. Any way, I think you were telling me that we were going some where." Annie smiled.

"Yes, that's right. Well, the reservation is about a six-hour ride away, and we can stay with my folks for the weekend. If anyone asks, then tell them you have a class trip of some kind. Hopefully, we should manage to get everything worked out in one weekend, but the doc will always be there, and he loves to help girls in distress, so even if it takes ten trips, we'll get to the bottom of things." He assured her.

"Great." She looked at him, a slight look of worry on her face. "Do I have to pay something to see this guy?"

"Nah, as I said, the doc loves to help. I gave him a quick description, and he seemed really interested to meet you." He told her, hoping he was right. "Anyway, I'll leave you to it. I'm sure you have important things to get done."

She led him out, and as he walked away from her door, he did feel slightly elated. Then he remembered that she apparently had a date that night, and his heart sank just a little.

Chapter Seven

She hadn't expected to see him again so soon. When he had shown up at her door, she had almost imagined he had come to ask her out, but quickly realised that there was no way that he could. After all, he *was* her teacher. And yet there he was. There he had been, while her brother was talking as loudly as he could about something that Annie would rather have not told him about. Her date.

His name, apparently, was Harley. Carlene would have a lot to answer for if he turned out to be a dud, especially now that André had reminded her, so rather loudly, about the date in front of Matthew Wilkins. She could've killed him when he said it. The last thing she wanted was for Matthew to think that she was dating widely. Although, she did have to admit that if he got the notion she was, it might just make him aware that she was, in fact, very definitely a female.

Actually, she wasn't dating widely, anyway. She had simply been set up with Carlene's brother. And since Carlene had been dating André for eighteen months, there was little chance that André didn't think it was a fantastic idea. Of course, the fact that Harley was Carlene's brother could lead to disaster all by its self. He was Carlene's *younger* brother, which meant he was, in fact, younger than Annie was. Plus, he was in from out of town, and probably didn't really want to be set up any more than she did.

As she sat at her desk, trying to pull her face together, she looked back at the day reflectively. She had revealed all her secrets to Matthew. They were secrets that no one else knew, although she suspected that Gary had some idea of the truth, for he was always willing to accept her knowledge unquestioningly. His only problem was his reluctance to be set up with Jalena, the girl who worked at the coffee house. She could see that they were meant to be together, and had watched him looking longingly every time they were in there, which was often. He was simply being stubborn, knowing that André would not approve of him dating a girl who had chosen work instead of college after high school.

She had been trying, yet again, to convince him to ask her out when Matthew had driven out of the grocery store parking lot. Either he had serious engine problems, or he had been angry about something. She supposed, momentarily at least, that he might have seen her with Gary, and got the wrong idea. She did, of course, disregard the idea within moments of having it, knowing that Matthew would not react like that over her. Now, that bitch Ali Rice on the other hand, guys always reacted like that over *her*. If it weren't for the fact that she was dating one of her best friends, Annie would have ignored Ali all together. After all, though, she had known Barry Oakland since they were fourteen, and she and André had befriended him instantly. He did, after all, fit perfectly into the group, taking his place within her life, as she had always known he one day would. Still, when Ali turned up a few days into the first semester of freshman year, she was not so eager to accept her in. Barry had started dating her almost straight away, but Annie could not like her.

It was true, Annie hadn't been dating much since she had first spotted Matthew Wilkins, but that was as much to do with the dreams, as they were to do with him. For as he arrived, the dreams had become more constant. They had always been there before, but slightly more sporadically than recently. Now they were at the point where they were occurring every night. That had never been the case before. As well as the frequency with which she was having the dreams, she had also realised that they had intensified, getting stronger and more real than ever before. At times, she was sure she could feel the ground shaking beneath her. There was now a sense of urgency that came with the dreams, that time was running out. She wanted to warn everyone, but she was merely a spectator within them, viewing all through another's eyes.

She was meeting this guy Harley at the coffee house at 7pm, then later they were, as André had reminded her so loudly, to meet her brother and Carlene at the movie theatre. This was really worrying her, because she would end up having to spend a couple of hours in the dark with him. Carlene was nice enough, but she couldn't imagine that she was going to hit it off with Harley.

Of course, she now had the knowledge that she was going away for the weekend with Matthew Wilkins. If nothing else got her through the next few hours, that thought was sure to. It was the ultimate chance for her to try and get close to him. And it had to make her wonder slightly, because it would be risky for him to be socialising with her. She had realised that already, but something told her that things were all right. Things were a part of who they were, not that she could tell him that. There was a six-hour drive to where they were going, so there was plenty of time for her to figure out how she was going to make her move during it. If all went well, she would be able to convince him of who she was, and by the end of the weekend, she would be close enough to touch him. For that was what she wanted most of all. To be close enough to him to touch him, to kiss him goodnight and hold his hand. It was supposed to be for them, she just had to convince him. After all, she had been dreaming of him since she was seven years old.

Maybe he already knew the truth. She had to believe it was possible, because she was not the only person in the world who slept and dreamt. And he knew about the dreaming mind, or so he claimed. On some level, she believed, he must know. But he chose not to see it. Or perhaps he did see it, but was merely unable to act. Worse than that, he may not wish to act. What if he realised the truth, but just *wasn't* interested. That would have been dreadful. It made her feel sick, knowing that she had found him, but may never get to posses him.

She sat in front of the mirror, trying to convince

herself that she must be wrong. He did not realise. That's all there was to it. She tried to occupy herself, curling her lashes, combing her freshly washed hair. She changed her mind several times on what to wear, finally deciding on jeans and a lace shirt she had been given by a cousin the summer before. It was slightly too lose on her now, because she had lost weight fairly steadily over the past year and a half. Her body had finally matured, and she had not even had to change her habits. Of course, she had been living in dorms, eating rice for the most part, and trying to remember where her next class was. Her skin had matured, too. It no longer felt the need to break out into red blotches or spots whenever she had a date, or felt particularly stressed by the workload piled upon her. Of course, she hadn't had so many dates just recently, but that was neither here nor there.

Joanna had quizzed her unashamedly when Matthew had gone. Questions about whom he was and what he wanted. Comments on who he was and what he looked like. Annie wouldn't tell her the real reason he had dropped round, and had given her a story about going on a class field trip at the end of the month. She had lied that she was just getting some last minute details about what she would need for the trip. Joanna seemed to swallow what Annie was telling her, and eventually let the issue drop. Annie wasn't about to tell her the truth about him.

André had seemed disinterested when she had introduced them. This had disappointed her slightly. He was going to be a part of her future. She had hoped that André would be happy, or at least a little interested. Matthew had seemed slightly relieved when she had introduced them. Perhaps he had thought she might be entertaining someone more influential than her brother. At least it did not seem that the two instantly disliked each other. This was pleasing, as Annie knew that they would at some point be the two most important males in her life.

7pm was fast approaching. Annie was dressed and ready to go by 6:30, but hesitated to make a move. In the end, she didn't leave her dorm room until 6:53. She didn't want to appear too eager, which she wasn't. For all she knew, Harley could have been a three-headed monster, or a nerd with black-rimmed spectacles, which would have looked much better on Buddy Holly. Worse still, he could be one of those jock types who spent all his time showing off his muscles to whoever would look at them. The thought of what he could be had to be worse than the reality, so she finally found herself pulling the door behind her, locking it, and making her way towards the coffee house.

As Carlene had suggested, Annie tied a red ribbon in her hair so that Harley would know who she was. She'd be able to tell who he was by his letterman jacket - so he must be a bit of a jock, after all. He was from out of state, so there was no way that any other person would have the same letterman jacket as he did.

She arrived at the coffee house at 7:02. There was no sign of Harley, so she ordered a hot chocolate, and took position in her favourite seat. At 7:09, the door to the coffee house swung open, and a guy in a green and black jacket entered the room. Annie knew as soon as she saw him that the idea of the blind date had been very bad. She prayed that there was a way out of it, because nothing she had imagined could have been so bad. She knew his blond hair and tall, slender frame. There was no mistaking him, because she had known him for too long. Every night, she fought as hard as she could to keep him from ever taking her dreams from her and the one she loved.

Chapter Eight

Her mouth hung open for a moment, until she realised that she had the look of shock on her face. He looked exactly as she knew he would, or should have known he would. Harley was the one that she feared the most when she slept. She knew his intentions toward her dream self, and how he intended to make them come to fruition. She did not know the name he had once had, but she did know him. The shortly cropped blond hair and brown eyes were even the same. He was so familiar to his dream counter part that it was like her dreams were coming true more now than ever. André, Gary, Barry, Ali, Carlene, Jalena, Matthew, herself. Harley was the missing piece that had so far eluded the group. The only problem was, she didn't want Harley to be there.

So now, here she was faced with Harley. When

Matthew had arrived at the college, she had known instantly that he would be there for her if she needed him. He had been like a breath of fresh air to her, because she finally felt that she was fully alive. But Harley was going to change all of that. She had known him too well before.

Now, as Annie sat in her favourite easy chair, clutching her hot chocolate, she could do nothing. She was dumbstruck as he crossed the room toward her. She felt nausea, foul tasting, in her throat. She wanted to throw up, but she could not move to do so. He was still walking toward her, and seemed to be taking forever to get there. Everything had slowed down, like in a movie action sequence where everything moves at less than half the speed it should do. Finally, things sped up again, as he offered her his hand, and introduced himself.

"Hi, I'm Harley." He introduced, as if she had not been able to tell who he was without being told. She tried to smile politely, but got the feeling it came out as more of a grimace. It definitely wasn't the smile she offered Matthew whenever she saw him. Harley sat down in the same spot where Matthew had sat only days before, and continued to speak in a rapid voice which sounded about as nervous as she had felt before she had even seen him. "You wouldn't believe how nervous I was walking over here tonight. I thought I was going to turn and run away most of the way, but here I am, and still nervous as anything. Carlene told me you were pretty- and she wasn't kidding- and normal, so I figured I had nothing to worry about, but it just made it worse. Carlene and André are pretty tight, though. And they make such a nice looking couple, don't you think?"

"They're soul mates." Annie told him. He didn't look as if he believed her for one moment, but she knew the truth. *He talks too much,* she thought. She sighed, and wondered how long it would take her to reach the door if she ran. She realised, though, that there was no way she would be able to do that. It wasn't the way that she was, the way that she had ever been. She had never hidden away. Even during the days after the death of her father, she had not stayed curled up in bed like her brother had, or cried silent tears in the den like her mother had. She had continued with her normal life. It was all a long time ago now, but she had not changed. The dreams had started only weeks later, and they had changed the way she saw the world. Harley was still talking.

"I never could understand the way Carlene could manage to date so many guys at the same time. I mean, I can go for months without a date, but Carlene? She's never happy unless she has at least a couple guys hanging on at the same time. Not that I think she'd cheat on André, because I think she's fairly faithful to him. In fact, I think she may even be ready to settle down for a while. Like I said before, they do make such a nice looking couple. I like André; he's a great guy. I think she's devoted to him, at the moment at least." He continued. Annie sighed again, more loudly this time, and wished that she had a trap door through which she could escape. Then, as she scanned the room to see where the emergency exit was, she spotted Matthew coming in. She beckoned him over, Harley didn't even notice as he continued talking. Matthew was on his way over to her, but then he spotted Harley, and started to leave instead. Annie couldn't bear the thought of the evening with Harley stretched before her, and sprang out of her seat to call out to him.

"Mr. Wilkins! Hi, come and join us." She called to

him. Perhaps it was the expression on her face, or the tone of her voice, but he smiled at her reassuringly, and squeezed his way between a couple of tables full of students to reach them. She mouthed the words thank you, and wondered exactly how she would introduce them, and what she would do when Harley realised that she was giving him the brush off. "Matthew, I'd like you to meet Harley. His sister Carlene is dating André at the moment. Harley, this is Matthew Wilkins."

"Hi." Matthew acknowledged the other male dully, although the smile was still on his face. Close up, she could tell it was not the most sincere smile in the world. He sat down on a wooden chair turned back to front, and Annie realised that he didn't look all that impressed at having been bought into the situation. She offered him a smile, and he returned it instantly. She felt in that smile the same electricity she felt every time their dream counterparts came together. It was the same feeling she had felt the first time she had seen him, the same feeling she had had when he first spoke directly to her in the auditorium only a few days earlier. But she sensed that it was nothing compared to the way it would feel if she ever managed to touch him. She watched him for a long moment, before turning to look at Harley, who, she realised, had rather remarkably fallen silent at last. The expression on his face was slightly dejected as he stood up.

"I'm going to get a drink. Would you like anything, Annie?" He asked. She showed him the cup in her hand, which was still half full, although now rather less than hot. "Oh, right, well, I won't be a moment."

Annie watched him walk away, and sighed with relief. "Oh, God! I didn't think he was ever going to shut up. I've never heard anyone talk so much about nothing. Thank you so much for coming to my rescue."

"Who is he, anyway?" Matthew asked, looking over at the counter where Harley seemed to be trying to get Jalena's attention, without much success.

"A blind date gone terribly wrong. Matthew, I *know* this guy, if you get my meaning. He's going to become obsessed with me, even though I already know I am going to hate him. If I don't put a stop to things now, I'm never going to get away from him, and I really can't take the idea of that. I don't care if my brother *is* dating his sister, I am *not* supposed to date him." She told him. His expression told her he understood without having it spelt out for him.

"So, is Harley his real name?" Matthew asked, a mischievous look in his eyes.

"Don't! I can't believe I agreed to be set up on this date in the first place. If André had any idea of my dreams, then I would march over and tell him right now just how bad a thing it was that he try to set me up with the one male soul on the entire planet that I am pretty sure I want nothing to do with. I'm really not sure I can wait another three weeks to find out the truth, but I *am* sure that I don't want to spend them any where near him." She told him. The look in his eyes changed, although she could not pinpoint what it had changed to.

"I'll take it that this is not who the dream you is growing close to. So, I'm guessing, somewhere along the line, someone has decided that you are supposed to be with him instead, but no one is paying attention to the fact that you're in love with someone else." Matthew surmised, looking over at the counter again. "He seems to be getting somewhere, so he should be back in an hour or two. Actually, if my hunch about the dates of your dream land turns out to be right, then you were probably matched to his soul by some star chart which gave the most advantageous matches. You wouldn't have had any say in the situation, and if you did, then you probably ended up being ignored. I have no idea of how they ever thought that it would work! I guess that modern arranged marriages work, but they aren't normally agreed at birth, and decided by the phase of the moon and the position of the stars."

"I take it you believe in love, then." She smiled.

"I believe in many things, Annie. What I believe most of all is that if the soul is searching for someone in particular, then it sometimes gets lucky. You have been incredibly lucky to find a number of souls that are linked directly to your own, so it stands to reason that you should find the one that means the most to you. If Harley has been a problem for your soul in the past, then I would guess that he will probably *still* be a problem." He told her, glancing at the counter once again. "He's coming back. May I recommend making a dash for it? I'll keep him busy if you like."

"There's no way I'm leaving you here with him. He'd probably pump you for information on me, and you know far too much." She told him, not letting on that her real worry was that Harley may well attack Matthew. As Harley came closer, a young girl stepped on to the small stage at the front of the room, about to start reading her poetry. He was clutching a large cup close to his chest, trying very hard not to spill any of its contents, while also trying to sit down on the chair he had been sitting in before. As he did so, the poetess started to read. Unfortunately, her first line, 'stand up', was delivered with such ferocity, that Harley shot back up again. The cup that he was holding could not keep hold of the liquid, and half of it ended up on the letterman jacket he was still wearing.

Annie tried hard to conceal her laughter, although a few giggles crept out. Matthew, on the other hand, made no such attempt, and laughed rather loudly. Harley glared at him, which really only made things worse. Sadly, the young poetess was getting rather flustered by the laughter, and in the end she ran off the stage, tears running down her face. All of a sudden, there were many more people looking at them, mostly all glaring rather angrily at Matthew. Annie wished that the trapdoor she had hoped would appear could now be big enough for both of them to escape through.

"I'm sorry, you're either going to have to be quiet or leave." Jalena told Matthew, coming over to the place where they were sitting. There was no way he was shutting up, so instead he looked at Annie, gave her an apologetic smile, and got to his feet. It took all of two hundredths of a second for Annie to decide that she was going with him.

They left Harley there, sitting covered in coffee. Annie wondered momentarily why he hadn't followed them, but as she walked beside Matthew back toward the dorms, all thoughts of Harley disappeared from her mind.

Chapter Nine

Harley was madder than he had ever been in his life. She had run off with that guy! Something inside of him wanted to hurt her, hurt them both, for embarrassing him. How dare she react like that to his misfortune? She was another one of those types of girls that thought they were above him. He had seen it far too many times before.

When he had first seen her, he had felt that it was right, that he had met the girl that would change the misfortune that he had experienced in the past. He felt almost as if fate was bringing them together. Then that other guy had turned up! True, that other guy was probably better looking than he was, but he couldn't see that they were actually an item. After all, she wouldn't have agreed to a date with him if she was dating some one else, would she? He would have to talk to Carlene about this one, he decided, as he used paper napkins to mop the coffee off his jacket. It would smell bad for a while, but the black fabric of the jacket would hide any stains.

He tried to settle back, to relax a little, but he felt a bit like an idiot. They had gone too far. How dare she do that to him? She was probably one of those girls who fooled around with people's emotions. That would be just his luck! He had dated girls like that in the past, and he had always made it perfectly clear that it wasn't okay. He wouldn't let this one get away with it. He would bide his time, before he made his move, though.

That was when he noticed the girl who was watching him. She was a pretty thing, blond, attractive, well built in front. She looked about the same age as him, and a little familiar. When she smiled at him, he felt a flicker of recognition. She stood up, and slid across the room towards him. Even the way she moved was attractive. The dress she was wearing was so tight it left almost nothing to the imagination, pale blue, less than knee length. He gulped back some of his coffee, and tried to look relaxed.

"Hi, I'm Ali." She smiled coyly at him. "I saw you with Annie before. Can you believe she is actually willing to be seen in public with that guy? I mean, teachers are not a good catch, are they."

"That guy was a teacher?" Harley asked in surprise. The guy didn't even look old enough to teach kindergarten.

"Oh, he looks young, alright, but he is most definitely faculty. Everyone knows it must be dumb to date the teacher, not that they can be dating, I'm sure. Although, I wouldn't put anything past Annie Bouvais.

She has a talent for doing the wrong thing. I mean, she did just walk out on you, didn't she? Of course, that guy is pretty hot property in the teacher's lounge, they say. All the spinster teachers have a thing for him, 'cause he *is* young. But she isn't allowed to date him, and besides, why date the guy who gives out the homework, right? Right. Of course, he teaches anthropology, so that apparently makes him more interesting, but for God's sake, he acts like a 60 year old trig teacher most of the time." Ali told him, speaking a mile a minute, as she sat down in the chair that Annie had relinquished. "What's your name? You didn't tell me."

"I'm Harley." He told her, trying to ignore the rapidity with which she spoke. He was already wondering how he was going to manage to get her out of that dress, because he wasn't convinced it did her justice.

"Not Davidson?" She asked, giggling in a way that suggested she was trying to act as if she was shy, and not the centre of attention that he had already figured out she probably was. He had heard the joke so many times that he no longer found it even remotely funny. All the same, he was not about to let on that he had a very small sense of humour.

"No, not Davidson." He laughed gently at her joke. "Well, I was just about to get another drink. Would you like something?"

"Coffee would be good, thanks." The girl replied. He stood and made his way over to the counter, which was much quieter than it had been the last time he went to it. He asked the waitress who had told that guy to stop laughing for a couple of coffees, and she told him she would bring them over to them. Heading back to where Ali was sitting, he thought things were starting to look up at last. He sat down, and she looked at him for a moment before asking: "So, how long have you known Annie?"

"About half an hour or so. I'm gonna kill my sister for setting me up on this date. Her brother is dating my sister, and she thought it would help me get to know the area if I went out with that girl. I can't believe I let myself get talked into it. We seemed to be doing okay, then that Wilkins guy came along, and the damned girl smiled for the first time all evening." He replied angrily, again vowing that she wasn't going to get away with it.

"That figures. They would deny it, no doubt, but I reckon there's something going on between those two. I've seen the way he looks at her. And as for little Miss Perfection, well, she is always out to go one better than the rest of us. How he can stand it, I'll never know." Ali acknowledged.

"I can tell there's something there. I try never to get involved when it's obvious a girl is with someone else. I'm guessing you've got a guy on the go. After all, a pretty thing like you can't have any shortage of offers." Harley said, feeling rather awkward, but wanting to know the answer despite himself. Actually, he had already decided it didn't matter one way or the other.

"Well, I've been seeing a guy named Barry for a while, but he's never really given me what I want. I've been on the look out for some fresh meat for a while, if you catch my drift." She told him. Her meaning was so obvious that even a blind man would have seen it. She winked at him, and he smiled back at her. This seemed even more like destiny than his meeting with Annie had been. This was what he had been waiting for, his reason for leaving Seattle to come here. He had been working toward this point in his life ever since it had started.

"Well, how about we do this more often? I just moved from out of town, and I'm staying in a motel while I get something more permanent sorted out. Maybe you'd like to come visit. After all, it gets a little lonely there all by myself." His words were as full of meaning as hers had been. He normally would have been embarrassed by them, but for some reason, this girl made him feel completely at ease.

"How about tonight?" She suggested.

"Why not."

"Yeah, after all, it *is* Saturday night. I don't have anywhere to be tomorrow, and I could do with a late night. It could be just what I need."

The waitress put two cups of coffee on the table between them, apologising about how long it had taken for them to be made. Harley was barely even listening to her though. He could almost taste the girl next to him. They didn't bother to drink the coffees. Instead, Harley led Ali back to his motel room, where they spent the entire night together.

Chapter Ten

As Matthew walked her back to her dorm room, Annie felt that she was floating on air. They had escaped the coffee house, and made their way to a burger place just off campus, where they had hoped they wouldn't be seen by anyone who might incriminate them. They had talked for a long while. Annie had told him a lot about her life, and he had told her more about his childhood, although there still seemed to be gaps. He had told her how his father was a doctor, and how he had practically grown up on the reservation after they had moved to a close by town. His father had worked closely with the people on the reservation, and Matthew had quickly become a part of the scenery. His friend, Brandon, had shown him all the sights, and together they had spent their days exploring the surrounding lands.

He had decided to go into teaching when he was fourteen. His parents had taken him on a journey to South America, where he had first seen the Mayan temples. They had impressed him so much, that he had started to read everything he could about them. He had moved on to the Egyptians, which he found even more thrilling, because of all the mystery and magic they were associated with. He had consumed every book he could find on the subject, and by the end of the summer, he knew almost as much as someone who had studied the subject for their entire lives. He hadn't realised until then how much history there was on his own doorstep, and now his explorations with Brandon were far more focused. In the end, he became almost like an apprentice to an elder from the reservation, and he had, again, gathered all the knowledge that was there to be gained. Then he realised that there was a way that he could share all the knowledge with others if he dedicated his life to teaching.

After that, he'd had to devote himself to his studies, so much so that he almost abandoned all other pursuits. When he admitted to Annie that he had barely even managed to date during high school, she had watched his face turn a gentle shade of red beneath his early spring tan. Annie found it all incredibly touching, that he had spent all these years learning just so that he could give his passion to others. And now, here he was, sharing it with her.

All too soon, though, they were back out side her dorm room. Even though she had tried to walk as slowly as possible, the evening had not lasted for anywhere near long enough. They had been talking for hours now, but it still wasn't enough for her. She wished she could just have another hour, but it was over already, and it was time to say good night.

"Would you like to come in for a coffee?" She asked, hoping that he would say yes, but realising that there was little chance of it.

"I would, but I don't think it's wise." He replied, his voice sounding disappointed with himself. "How about I take a rein check?"

"Sure, maybe when we go down to the reservation, if you still think that's a wise idea." She told him, trying to sound light, but not quite keeping the worry from her voice.

"Look, I don't want for you to worry about anything, okay? I'll admit, there would be raised eyebrows if the faculty discovered that you and I were becoming friends rather than teacher and pupil, but the problem would be mine. Relax, Annie, please. The only thing I think we shouldn't broadcast is that I'm taking you on a six hour drive to my parents' house for the weekend." Matthew laughed. She had to admit, she had been worried, but his tone made her feel much more at ease about everything. "Now, please, go get some sleep. Good night, Annie. Don't let your dreams get in the way."

"Good night, Matthew. I'll see you Monday, if not sooner." She smiled. He smiled back at her momentarily, before walking away down the hall toward the stairways which would take him back downstairs and out into the night. Annie cursed herself quietly as she unlocked the door and stepped into the living room area. Inside, Joanna was watching an old movie, something with Judy Garland and Mickey Rooney as far as she could tell. It was not until that point that she remembered the movie she and Harley were supposed to see with Carlene and her brother.

"Hey, the wanderer returns!" Joanna exclaimed when she spotted Annie. "André called, said something about a movie. I guess he figured you and your date had something better to do. So, where have you been with the guy?"

"What, Harley? I, uh, I ditched him at half past seven, in the coffee house." Annie admitted. "He embarrassed himself rather badly, and I had no choice but to leave him there."

"So, where *have* you been?" Joanna persisted.

"Well, I went for something to eat with Matthew Wilkins." Annie informed her friend, sitting down on the couch next to her. Joanna looked at her for a moment, then shook her head in disbelief.

"Okay, what's the 411? I know there's something going on here." Joanna pushed.

"Well, like I told you earlier, he's my teacher, and he's arranging a field trip for a few of the class members. I happen to be one of those included. I guess we just got talking far too easily, and I completely lost track of the time."

"Who else is going, then?"

"Brad Martins and Cara Driver, from my anthropology group. I don't think you know them." Annie lied. The two names she had given had dropped out of her class at the beginning of the semester.

"When will it be? I'll invite Curt up for the weekend." Her roommate told her.

"Last weekend of the month, as far as I know. Any way, it's getting late and I'm tired to the point of no return. 'Night."

Annie went into the bedroom, undressed in the dark, and climbed into bed. She lay looking out of the window, wondering how far Matthew had got toward his own apartment. She knew she was playing a dangerous game, that she could end up getting Matthew fired if she wasn't careful. The reality of the situation worried her, but at the same time, she had no desire to stop the friendship that was starting to grow between them. She liked being close to him too much to stop. Yet, at the same time, she knew she was going to have to slow down the rapidity with which it was growing. She couldn't let him take all the responsibility if they did get caught.

Not that there was really anything to catch. He *was* only a friend. She knew that there was plenty of time for her to show him the truth about their destinies, but for now they were only friends. He *had* called them friends, hadn't he? If the faculty had a problem with the teachers being friends with their pupils, then that was their problem. But it really wasn't. It wasn't okay for Annie to socialise with him, and she was going to have to stop herself from finding ways to do so.

In the distance, she watched as a light came on, and wondered who it may be. Matthew would be home by now, and she imagined that he was out there somewhere, wondering what she was doing. A few minutes passed, and the light went out. There were suddenly no street lamps, and the air was suddenly still and warm. Annie was barely aware that she had started to dream.

She was in the dark again, and she could hear voices talking to her once more. Then, finally, she was outside, with him. They spent a perfect day together, but the day ended with bad news. Then the day again, and she was in the woods with the one she loved, but then her brother came, and the two men had a fight. Her brother's friend consoled her. The other girl came out of the woods, trying to join the argument, and her voice brought the arrival of the other boy, the one she did not like. It was all because she had fallen in love with someone she was not even supposed to look at.

Suddenly, the ground was shaking. Everyone started to scream, except for the girl, and her brother's friend. They were expecting it. Then the ground was still again, and all eyes turned to her. They believed that she was the one making the ground shake. They wouldn't believe that she was not able to make it happen. She was crying, but he held her to his chest. Then, she could feel hands upon her, pulling her from his arms.

Annie woke up to the sound of her own screams. Joanna was standing over her bed, shaking her arm gently, trying to wake her up.

"Annie, Annie! Wake up for Christ's sake. What the hell's going on?"

"I'm sorry, I just had a nightmare is all. I'll be fine now, go back to bed." Annie told the other girl. She was sure she could still feel the hands of the guards on her arms, and thought that if she checked under the sleeves of her nightshirt that she might find the marks that their hands had left. She could still see the anger in her brother's eyes as he had helped the guards to drag her to the isolation chamber for another night.

"Are you sure you're alright? You really don't look so good." Her friend asked in concern.

"I'm fine. I guess I should stop reading those horror novels before bed." Annie told her, hoping that her voice was sounding even, and that the panic had left it now. Her roommate finally gave in and went back to bed. But there was no way that Annie could sleep again now. She had felt the quake, and knew that the safety of her dreamland was no longer sure. The danger was growing more imminent now with every passing moment.

Instead, Annie lay awake for the rest of the night, staring out of the window to where the light had appeared earlier in the night, pretending that it was Matthew, and that he could feel her anxiety. Silently, she waited for dawn to arrive. Sunday morning bought a trip home with André, Gary and Barry, for a large dinner, which her mother loved to cook. Her cousins may be there, too, making their usual jokes, which were about as funny as fleas. But at least it would take her mind off things. She lay and waited for the shatter of dawn, and when it finally came, she did the only thing she knew of that would calm her thoughts. She went running.

Chapter Eleven

Annie was at the back of the auditorium again. He could see her from where ever he stood down at the front. Her face looked unhappy, and he hoped that he would get the chance to talk to her, to make sure she was all right. She didn't look it, and he was a little worried. Although he had told her not to worry about anything, he wasn't sure that she hadn't been.

His lesson felt dull to him, but he ploughed on through it, because he had been set the plan by an over baring head of department. Apparently, it had got back to that same head of department that Matthew's lessons weren't quite as academically based as they should be. It all seemed very dry, and he actually realised that most of the things he was telling them were way beneath their understanding of the subject matter. He couldn't wait until he was actually fully qualified, and no one would make such demands on his educational aspirations.

He kept looking at the clock, checking just how long he had to continue teaching this drivel that was, in places, highly inaccurate, and downright misleading. But there was still another half hour, and he had lost a couple of the slackers who sat at one side of the stage. He was pretty sure he could hear snoring coming from somewhere. Worst of all, a glance up to the back of the room showed him that he had even lost Annie's attention, now.

"You know something, guys, this is too much. It's a nice day out, so, just sit tight for another ten minutes, and then you can go. And if it turns out that I'm not allowed to tell you some true facts in the next lesson either, well, we'll think of something else." He told them finally, with twenty-five minutes left to go. The head of department would just have to give him a ticking off. "Talk amongst yourselves."

The auditorium broke into chatter, and Matthew turned to the board, erasing the rubbish from its surface. He would've gone to the head of department and told him where to shove his lesson plans, but his fear got the better of him, because despite himself, he was getting more and more caught up in the idea of Annie Bouvais. She was still up at the back, and she seemed to have actually fallen asleep, now.

Matthew turned to his teaching aid, and flicked it open to the particular subject that he had just been teaching. As he expected, the facts that he had been asked to teach were so far out of date that they were now discussed as a joke amongst the more up to date texts. He was just about to tell the rest of the students to leave when he realised that there were moans coming from the back, from Annie. The chatter started to quieten, as the moans got louder. Finally, there was a loud scream, and everyone turned to look at her.

He was by her side within seconds, and as she started to slide out of her seat, he caught her and righted her. She still seemed to be sleeping, but she did not stir at the movement.

"Annie?" He asked, realising that there was far too much concern in his voice. He knelt on the floor next to her, and tried to wake her. When she didn't make any response, he turned to the girl on the other side of the auditorium steps. "Please could you go and find the nurse, she's in the office at the end of the corridor from the top steps."

The girl took the door that was only feet from her, and he turned back to Annie. She seemed to have stopped moaning. Up close, he could see just how pale she really was. Now he was really starting to worry about her. The rest of the students were chattering about her, except for Ali, who was sitting in the front row, still managing to laugh and flirt with the guy she was sitting next to. The other girl, whose name Matthew would have to learn now, returned, the nurse behind her, bustling as campus nurses usually did. She pushed Matthew out of the way, and seemed to be checking all her vital signs. Matthew didn't know what else to do, so he turned to the rest of the auditorium.

"I think we'll leave things there for now. Please, read chapters 18 and 19 for the next class, and try to forget everything I just taught you, because it was all wrong." He told the class, which got laughs from many of the other students. They all started to gather their things, and left the auditorium via the lower doors. Once they were all gone, Matthew turned back to the nurse. "Is it something serious?"

"I don't think so. This poor lamb just needs some rest, and a damned good meal. Could you be a dear and carry her to my office, I think she'd be more comfortable on the bunk in there until she wakes up." The nurse assured him.

Matthew felt decidedly uncomfortable with the situation, but he did as was asked. He scooped her up in his arms, and carried her to the nurse's office. As he laid her on the bed, and the nurse dismissed him, he couldn't stand the feeling of helplessness that seemed to overwhelm him.

Chapter Twelve

She could have died when she realised what she had done. It was so embarrassing, falling asleep in class, and worse than that, they'd had to call the nurse in to make sure she was all right. By all accounts, or rather by the account of Bonnie, the girl who had been sent to get the nurse, Matthew Wilkins had seemed very worried about her. She would have asked Gary, but he'd been out sick for the day, and she wasn't even sure he had heard about the episode.

When she had finally woken up in the slim bunk in the nurse's office, she had no idea where she was, or how she had gotten there. The nurse had treated her as if she were really very unwell, and had recommended that she go and see a doctor as soon as possible. Annie said that she would, but knew that the only doctor she would be seeing was the hypnotherapist that Matthew was taking her to see.

She was starting to worry, though. The fact was, Matthew had seemed worried about her, so she was going to have to do her best to avoid him unless absolutely necessary. She had no other choice, now. If it killed her, she would manage to keep away from him.

As she lay awake at night, all she could hope was that she was prolonging their days, that she was giving them more time, and that she would be able to find out what happened to her soul all those years ago. It was only a couple of weeks now before she would find out. She had to give them more time.

Chapter Thirteen

She was ignoring him, he could tell. It was the only thing he could think of that made any sense. He would have voiced his concern, but he wasn't sure whom he should voice them to. The school nurse had informed him that she had been absolutely fine, but that she had recommended a trip to the doctor. He had thought that he might go to the nurse, but the thought lasted less than a few moments. His next thought was to talk to André or Gary, but he didn't know either of them well enough to talk to them. Besides, her brother had absolutely no idea about her dreams, or so she had told him. He didn't know any of her other friends, really. Maybe he should talk to her.

He had taken to watching her in the mornings. The first time, he had spotted her by accident, when he'd had to get up rather too early in order to fix the lesson plan he had been given by the department head. He had been pacing, as he tended to do when he was particularly frustrated, and there she had been, running on the track that circled the field just beyond his window. He had trained the telescope on her, and bought her to within inches of his reach. The next morning, he had set his alarm for dawn, and ran to his telescope to see if she was out again. And there she had been. By the end of the week, his mild concern for her had grown into full-blown worry. He wanted to talk to her instead of just watching what was happening to her.

Perhaps, he thought, her dreams were keeping her awake. He had assumed that her scream was something to do with her dreams, but he had not had the chance to ask her. *She'll kill herself if she's not careful*, he thought to himself. That frightened him immensely, because he wasn't allowed to be worried about her, because he was a teacher and she was his pupil, and that was not allowed. He couldn't take the thought of anything happening to her.

But he didn't have time for thinking. He had an eight o'clock class to take, and it was 7:45 already. If he didn't get a move on, he would be in more types of trouble than he already was. He pulled on his t-shirt, and grabbed his keys before racing out of the apartment. He made his way down to the parking lot, and climbed into his car, trying to figure out what he was supposed to do. He pulled into the faculty parking lot with a few minutes to spare.

He did his best to struggle through the lesson, because he had to, holding together for as long as it took. It was Friday already, and he hadn't spoken to her all week. The lesson was more interesting than some of the others had been, as they looked at a tribe of people who had lived in the Amazon, cut off from the rest of the world. He tried to inject some humour into the words that he had been asked to read them, but it didn't really work.

Later that day, he had to go for his meeting with Jerry Hathaway. It was the same type of meeting as it always was. Jerry asked him a whole heap of questions: how were the students liking his lessons? How were they coping with the workloads? Were there any problems that he had? They were all answered the same way; everything was fine. The truth was, everything was far from fine, because he was starting to suspect that he had chosen the wrong path when he decided he was going to be a teacher. He had realised it fairly quickly, but something had kept him from letting on. He had come to realise that it was Annie.

Hathaway's office was three floors down from Annie's dorm room. When the meeting was finally over, he made the instant decision to go to see her. Making his way up the stairs, he wondered exactly what he was going to say to her when they were face to face, but it didn't matter what he said, because he was going to be there with her. Of course, as he knocked on the door, he wasn't so convinced that he hadn't made a mistake. The door was answered quickly, by the roommate.

"Hi, Joanna, right?" He smiled at the girl. She looked at him, and smiled back.

"Come back to see Annie, Huh? Well, she's in there. I think she may be resting, not that she sleeps so much anymore. I wondered if maybe she'd had a fight with a guy, but you're the first one who's come to see her, so I figure it must be the nightmares. God, I've never heard anyone scream in their sleep like that before." The girl spoke, her smile fading fast. "I hope she'll tell you more than she ever tells me."

"I'll let you know." He told her, and made his way over to the other door. Matthew knocked lightly, and waited for her voice.

"Come in." It finally called. As he pushed the door open, he waved back at the other girl. Inside, he found Annie, lying on the bed fully clothed, staring up at the ceiling. As he came in, she turned and looked at him. "Hi."

"Annie, what's the matter?" He asked gently, pulling a wooden chair up beside her bed. He could see now just how tired she looked. Her face had the look of someone who had stopped eating altogether, and her eyes seemed to have sunk into the sockets. They were still that intense green, but the sparkle had rather disappeared.

"Oh, there's nothing wrong, unless you count the fact that I haven't slept since Monday morning, which was an accident, by the way. I haven't eaten anything since Saturday evening, because the thought of food makes me feel sick, and I can barely stand the thought that tomorrow, my brother is making me go to this dumb surprise party, which I'm not supposed to know anything about. I mean, how stupid does he think I am?" She told him.

"Why aren't you sleeping?" Matthew probed gently.

"Because, alright? I'm sorry, but I'm not really in the mood for talking. I think you've had a wasted journey, Mr. Wilkins." She told him shortly. The use of his name like that made him feel devastated.

"Is it about the dreams, Annie?" He asked, trying to conceal his feelings about it.

"What do you think? Of course it's about the dreams. It's already starting. I'm running out of time, and it's already starting." She told him, looking back to the ceiling.

"What's starting?"

"The end! Don't you see? If I don't sleep, then I don't dream. If I don't dream, maybe I can give them more time, maybe I can save them all."

"Annie, it's the past, you can't stop it because it already happened."

"I know I can't stop it, but I have to slow it down. Maybe if I slow it down enough, then they can finish the ships they are building in Isis, maybe more of them will survive."

"Where is Isis?"

"I have no idea. I believe it's by the sea, but to be honest, that doesn't help me all that much. It's just; it's all too real. All of a sudden, it isn't enough to think of it as a dream any more. I am there, and I have no idea what is going to happen. I've heard those stories, you know, dreaming that you die and then you do? Well, what if it's true? What if I dream I'm dead, and I never wake up again?" She was starting to cry. "It's so real, Matthew. Please, help me."

"I'm here to help you, Annie." He tried to assure her, relieved to hear her use his first name. "I called the doc, and he can do next weekend instead if you like. I'm sorry that I can't change the past, but I think we can find out what happened so that we can stop it from repeating itself."

"So you don't think I'll die if I dream it?" Annie

asked, her face still looking worried.

"I think that's a myth, Annie." He told her gently. He could not keep the tenderness from his voice, as hard as he tried to. She was there, within his reach, and he could almost feel how much she needed him, feel the pain she was going through.

"I'm so scared, Matthew. In the last dream, they took me back to the isolation chamber. I can still feel their hands on me." She told him, sitting up and pulling the sleeve of her shirt up. He could see what appeared to be the shape of fingers bruised into her upper arm. "This isn't natural, Matthew. This is because of a dream! No one else has held my arm that tightly, so where else could it have come from? Now tell me that if I die in the dream I won't die in real life, too."

"I've never seen manifestation like that before, Annie." He admitted, looking closely at the bruises, which had obviously been there for a while. They had started to turn yellow as they had aged. "But I still don't think that you can die just because you dream it. I know you're frightened, but you have to sleep, and eat something, please."

"I'm not sure I can." Her voice wavered. Matthew looked at her, wishing he could reach out to her, even for just a moment. It was almost as if she could read his mind, when she asked him: "Would you please hold me? I need to feel protected."

"Sure." He told her softly, knowing that if they were anywhere else, he would have had to say no. He tried not to sound too eager, making it clear that he realised that her need was to be held by anyone, and that he was merely the closest person to her at that moment.

He moved onto the bed beside her, and wrapped

his arms awkwardly around her. She softened toward him, melting into his arms so that he was barely able to tell where she stopped and he began. He held her for a minute, then another, reluctant to let her go, but all the while realising that he would have to. He could feel her tears seeping through his t-shirt as he cradled her gently in her arms, stroking her hair, soothing away her pain.

But all too soon, the minutes were over, and he had to let her go. Reluctantly, he withdrew his arms from around her body. The tears had stopped, but she continued to sniff. Matthew was stunned to realise how much Annie looked like a scared, innocent child. He wished he could tell her the truth, that he could tell her how he felt about her. But the words were not allowed, and he could not bring himself to break the rule that kept them unsaid. She was precious and vulnerable, and he could not put her in jeopardy by being selfish.

"Thank you." She whispered.

"I should probably get going now. Take care, Annie, and please sleep. We'll get all of this sorted out next weekend, but you need to sleep before then. If not for yourself, please, do it for me, because I really can't take the worry of keeping an eye on you while I'm trying to deal with those stupid lesson plans." He told her, trying to joke. She finally gave the slightest hint of a smile. "Believe me, if Professor Mitchell had his way, we'd all be learning information so out of date that we may as well be living fifty years ago."

"Well, that explains why when I compared my notes to the text all the facts were wrong. I didn't think you'd make those kinds of mistakes." She actually laughed a little.

"I know, tell me about it. I'll see you later, okay?"

He asked, hoping that this time he really would be able to talk to her again as soon as possible.

"Yeah, I'm so tired." She sighed.

"I know." He smiled at her. "Good bye, Annie."

He stood and started to leave. He turned back momentarily as he reached the door, and looked at her, offering her a smile. She returned it before turning her head, and closing her eyes. He noticed once more the look of exhaustion on her face, but he could not stay. He continued into the other room, where the other girl was sitting, watching TV, laughing at some joke that Matthew had missed the punch line to. She did not even notice him as he let himself out, and made his way back to his car.

Several hours later, he was back in his own apartment, and climbing into his own bed. He watched the dream catcher swaying in the doorway. A soft breeze was blowing through the open window. He had made the call to the doctor, and rearranged everything for the following week. Now he just had to get *through* the week

Sleep was evading him. He wished with all his heart that by giving up a night of his sleep that he was letting Annie rest peacefully, away from the dreams that stopped her from sleeping. Right now, he was exhausted, but not even remotely tired.

When he was young, Matthew had learned the secret of the dream catcher, and had been taught to respect the legends of the cultures that he had been raised with. However, even in later life, Matthew had sometimes had to question those beliefs. He had not been raised a Christian, and his father had encouraged him to find his own path to enlightenment. Now he found it increasingly difficult to believe in God, because what kind of god would allow Annie to suffer as she was.

Even so, he had to have some kind of faith, for he had managed to find Annie. For the first time ever, he realised that he had managed to fall in love. The only problem was, he wasn't allowed to love her. Even if she never loved him in return, he would always know that he had found her, and that she was the first girl he had ever loved. Too bad it was unrequited.

"Why can't I just tell her how I feel?" He asked out loud, more of a plea than a question. The words reverberated around the room as he sat up on the bed. "Why the hell can't I just tell her?"

Chapter Fourteen

Ali Rice was fast asleep. She and Harley had spent the best part of the week together. She knew she was being conniving, keeping Barry hanging on while she was sleeping with Harley, but to be honest, she really didn't care.

She'd woken at 9am with a bad headache, or maybe it was a hangover. She couldn't remember having been drunk the night before, but her memory wasn't fantastic some days. She knew she had been with Harley, and they had had good fun, until he'd had to run off to see his sister. She took a couple of aspirins, and waited for the headache to subside.

It was Saturday morning. Both Harley and Barry were going to a small get together for the Bouvais twins, which included that Annie girl. Harley was only going because his sister was dating André. But Barry! He actually liked that girl, as a friend! She had never understood that, because he had so much more potential than hanging around with Annie Bouvais. After all, he was one of the hottest athletes on campus. Still, he had asked her to come with him. She had decided when he asked her that she would, even if it was just to rub in Annie's face that she at least had a real boyfriend, where as she only had the merest of flirtations with Matthew Wilkins. Finally, she had decided it would be the perfect way for her to get Harley begging for more.

Her wardrobe was full of clothes that would make the right kind of statement, but she could not decide which one she would find the most productive. Her most fantastical was a little silver dress, so tight that it held her in and pushed her out in all the right places. The only problem with it was that it really wasn't suitable for the occasion. There was always her blue dress, but there was now a rather large tear in it where Harley had gotten a little over eager. When the clock read 10:30, and she was still dressed in nothing but her incredibly expensive underwear, she knew she was running late. Finally, she settled for pale blue Capri pants, and a white twin set. It was a classic look, she decided, as she piled her hair on top of her head. That just looked wrong, though, so she unpinned it, and it fell around her shoulders. She put in a couple of combs, and then set about fixing her face. A slick of black eyeliner over each lid, and a thin layer of pale lip-gloss were all she needed for the full effect to take shape. She looked in the mirror, and decided that she was a knockout.

"Oh what wicked webs we weave." The voice of Ali's roommate, Libby Fisher, came from the doorway.

"Scratch that. She's the devil in disguise. I like that a whole lot better."

"I'm going to a get together for those Bouvais twins. It's their birthday. I am not impressed, as it's supposed to be a surprise for Annie Bouvais. Barry is going to have to get over his thing for that girl. I mean, it's unnatural, the way he hangs around with her, but he claims there's nothing going on between them. Come on!" Ali told the other girl.

"So what about the other guy you got hangin' on?" Libby asked. She liked to think she was a southern belle. The southern part was true, at least. She was far too much of a tramp for anyone to consider her a 'belle', as far as Ali could tell. Ali shook her head in despair, and turned back to the mirror.

"Harley is giving me private lessons, or maybe I'm giving *him* the lessons. Well, at the moment, he is giving me exactly what I need, which Barry hasn't done for quite some time, if you really want to know." She told the other girl as she put a pale pink blush across her cheekbones.

"Well, if he is boring you, you could always pass him along the line. I would be more than willin' to take him off your hands. He's a nice lookin' boy." Libby smiled suggestively. Ali thought for a moment, before turning back to her.

"Well, why don't you drop by the frat house later, I'm sure we could get something worked out." Ali suggested, knowing that if she could pass Barry on, at least for a little while, she could concentrate on other activities instead.

"Sounds like a plan. See you later, sugar pie." Libby turned and sashayed out of the room. Ali didn't worry that Barry might get too attached to Libby. She was pretty enough, with redder hair than most bottles contained, and a rather remarkably slender frame. Ali didn't worry though, because she was the one who had the breasts (they had cost her father a small fortune, but they'd been a graduation gift). Her own hair was rather fantastically soft and blond, which had kept all the other girls in high school fairly jealous. Of course, Annie Bouvais had the kind of looks that Ali could only dream of. She was, actually, beautiful, while Ali realised she was merely attractive. Her dark hair was no real match for the blond, but it was thicker and fuller than Ali ever managed to achieve. Worse than that, she had those green eyes, so startlingly green that people could see them from a mile off. Annie's curves were all natural, although she couldn't be much more than a size six. It made Ali feel positively fat as a size eight. Plus, she had managed to capture the eye of Matthew Wilkins.

How he had decided to pick Annie Bouvais was beyond her. Ali should be the one to get him, not that prissy little cow. Still, she had got her own back on him. She had made it her personal mission to ruin his career. She'd started by telling Professor Mitchell that Matthew Wilkins did not know the first thing about anthropology. It had taken sleeping with the mouldy old fool to get what she wanted, but it had been worth it. Now she felt a little thrill whenever a fellow classmate fell asleep. Whenever she thought Mitchell would change his mind, she made sure he received the correct literature to keep him happy.

Barry had called her, and would be coming to pick her up shortly. She sat, waiting, listening to the CD he had burned her for Christmas. She was plotting. It was

Annie's birthday, and the party was in her honour, so there was no way that she wouldn't be there. Ali had to wonder whether Matthew Wilkins might be there. She realised even as she thought it that it was a stupid idea. There was no way that they would risk getting caught by someone. They were so awfully friendly with each other. All she had to do was look at the way he had reacted after her little episode in class. And she had also noticed the way he looked in her direction during classes, making sure he had her attention. She probably never took her eyes off him. Ali had even wondered whether they were sleeping together, but she had dismissed the idea within moments of having it, because she had decided long ago that Annie Bouvais was the kind of girl who was saving herself for marriage.

When Barry knocked on her door, she opened it for him, and greeted him with a kiss that was sure to make him want her madly. He told her how good she looked, and she blushed on cue. It was a talent she had discovered a long time ago, when she had played a bit role in a school play. Together, they walked across to the frat house, where the party was taking place. They were already a little late, and the surprise had already taken place.

The main room had been decorated with blue and yellow balloons, with '20 today' written all over them. There was a table covered in food and drinks. Underneath, there was a badly hidden crate of beers, just in case a faculty member *did* turn up. Some one else must know about Annie and Mr. Wilkins, Ali thought. Harley was already there, too. When he caught her eye, he gave her a wink. She smiled slightly, and put her arm around Barry as tightly as she could without arousing his suspicions. Watching Harley cringe gave her a great feeling of satisfaction, knowing that she was teasing him with her body language.

It didn't take her long to spot Annie Bouvais, standing over by the window, looking absolutely stunning in a long red dress, which hugged her figure, showing off her curves. Her dark hair was swept up into an intricate pattern of plaits and swirls. Her make up looked almost as if a professional had done it. She looked as if it was effortless to look so good. The only thing that she didn't have was someone with her. She was quite alone, there, and Ali's feeling of satisfaction grew stronger than ever.

"Hey, Ali, Barry, come on in and get a drink. Sodas on the table, beers underneath, and we have another two crates, so don't worry about how many you get through." Gary Hutchins greeted them. Ali wasn't keen on that guy, either, but she made an effort to smile and flirt just a little, as she took a diet soda, then started to mingle. As she made a beeline for Harley, she realised that she was going to have to introduce him to Barry.

"See you tonight?" Harley whispered in her ear. She nodded, and laughed a little. When Barry asked her later what he had said, she told him 'nothing much'.

When Annie finally moved away from the window, it was because Harley had asked her to dance. Ali could tell she agreed with reluctance, though. Ali watched with envy as Annie stepped out with most of the talents of a professional dancer, and several that were even better. By her side, Harley looked like a fool, but Ali knew he was only playing with her, teasing her like she had teased him.

When Libby had turned up, shortly before ten,

Barry had been so drunk that it had not been hard for her to get him to leave with her. That left Ali free to pursue Harley, and it didn't take long to convince him to leave with her. They managed to slip away without anyone else noticing, into the rainy night.

Chapter Fifteen

His voice came to me through the darkness once more. I was cold and frightened, but Malarchy's voice called in a whisper to me, calming me deep within.

"Anicia, I will be brief. They recalled the council. This quake has worried them, and they are all now convinced that the great quake will come soon. They say it will be within the next moon cycle. Niall told us we had more time, but we do not." Malarchy whispered to me.

"I know that to be true, for while I sit here, I can feel the ground shake beneath me. The gods are angry with us, they know that we have become savage, and that we do not deserve our land." I whispered in return, wishing that he could be within my arms.

"You are alright my love?"

"Of course, I am always. Although I now realise that if we are to stay here for the rest of the moon cycle, I will be joined to Haltar. I pray that the quake will come sooner, but I will be joined to him in half a moon cycle. There is not enough time between now and then. If we are not joined before the quake, then I shall go to the east, with you."

"I will wish for that to be so. Good night, sweet love, good night."

He was gone. The calm which had settled upon me remained throughout the night until morning. When I was finally released from the isolation chamber, I was taken back to the home temple, where I was dressed and made ready for the joining of Alim and Kylin.

Chapter Sixteen

Jalena Carmichael had worked all evening at the coffee house, hoping that tonight's tips might be enough to buy her a ticket home to see her parents. The place had been packed, as always, and she had spent hours carrying oversized coffee cups to people who had very little idea that there was a world outside college, one that they were someday going to have to live in. The full cups were emptied too quickly, and had to be replaced with new ones. Then there was the fun of the half eaten muffins, the bagels, that hadn't quite satisfied the fluffy chin boys, covered in rancid cream cheese. It was her least favourite part of the job, but she continued with it. Of course, there were the people who came in and went out without ordering anything. She rather liked them, because it kept her workload down. Sooner or later, most of the customers left to go and do other things, like going to the movies, or back to their dorm rooms. Jalena was left to tidy it all away.

Gary Hutchins had been in, at almost eleven. There had been a party for Annie and André, and although Annie had invited Jalena, she had known she couldn't attend because of work. Gary had been to the party, so she hadn't expected to see him, but there he was, ordering a coffee, and staying until all the other customers had vacated the place. She could tell he liked her. Plus, Annie had pointed him out to her. It was amazing, that within a week of starting the job at the coffee house, Annie had made friends with her. It was almost as if Annie had sought her out, making friends with her because she knew she should. Just recently, though, she seemed tired, as if she weren't sleeping at night.

As she left the coffee house, Jalena locked the door, and wrapped a scarf around her neck. It wasn't cold, but it had started to rain a couple hours earlier, and although it had started as a light drizzle, it was now fairly heavy. Jalena hugged herself against the wet air as she made her way around the side of the building, and up the stairs to the apartment she lived in. It wasn't luxurious, just a bedroom, living room, kitchen and bathroom. There was a fantastic roof terrace, though, which she utilised when the weather was fine. Better than that, though, it was her own space, even if she did share it with an over zealous cleaner of a cat named Rosencrantz.

"Hey, little kitty, are you hungry?" Jalena greeted him as she came through the door. He had been a gift from her parents shortly after she announced that she was moving out to go and work at the coffee house. She had been offered the job by her old boss, who had run the convenience store where she had worked since she was sixteen. The job included the apartment where she lived, and the pay was better than the convenience store, so she had packed up all her things and made a break for it.

The cat wound its way around her legs, mewing at Jalena as if he hadn't seen her in days. Jalena made her way into the kitchen, and pulled out a can of cat food, which claimed to be beef, but which smelt more like underpants and rotten goulash. As she put the food on the ground in front of the cat, she realised once again that she would be very lonely if it weren't for the fact that she had Annie Bouvais as her friend.

She made her way back into the living room, and curled herself up on the couch to watch some TV. *If Gary could see me now, he'd never ask me out* Jalena thought to herself, as she tried to pull her left shoe off. He was getting close to asking her out now, she believed, but he was just so slow about it. The gentle prods which Annie had been giving him were starting to work, finally, but it was still taking forever.

"She was trying to figure out whether she could be bothered to go to bed before she fell asleep or whether she could sleep where she was, when the phone rang. She waited three rings, knowing that at that time of night, it must be important. As she lifted it to her ear, she hoped it wasn't bad news. "Hello?"

"Jalena, honey, it's mom." The voice at the other end of the line told her.

"Hey, mom, what's wrong? You don't normally call so late." Jalena asked, not yet at ease.

"Nothing serious. You weren't home earlier, and I have been waiting for your father to fall asleep for the past half hour. It's his birthday on Monday, and I was hoping to bring him out there to see you. After all, you're so close, but we never get to see you these days." Her mother replied, making sure that Jalena would feel as guilty as possible.

"I know, mom, but I don't get much time to come home anymore, plus, I'm working on my tips stash to get there right now." She apologised.

"I know, honey. Anyway, if you could arrange for a cake, that would be really great. And we'll be there about seven."

"No problem, mom. I'll see you Monday, then." Jalena smiled as an idea occurred to her. "Bye, mom."

"Bye honey."

The idea had that occurred to Jalena was to get Annie to bring Gary to the coffee house. She looked around the apartment, and realised that she would have to spend the following morning pulling it into some kind of shape. But for now, she was trying to decide what she should wear, if she was going to try and get Gary to finally ask her out. She couldn't go too mad, because she had to save something for the eventual date.

She didn't work until 6 on Mondays, when she took over from the acne-ridden teenager, and a forty-year-old woman with a passion for poetry. Jalena was the manager, and loved the job, but she was always relieved when she got a few hours outside of the place. Of course, when she was there, she got to watch Annie's budding relationship with Matthew Wilkins. They were yet to do anything about it, but they did make the most perfect couple ever. It was even more obvious that they should be together than either of them was willing to admit to each other.

Right now, though, she was tired. She managed to pull herself out of her seat, and went to her own bed. Sleep came quickly, and so too did dreams. The dream was of herself, and Gary, and the others, too. Annie and Matthew were going to be married, but something happened to Matthew, and he was killed. The dream ended happily for Jalena at least, as she married Gary Hutchins. In her sleep, a smile crept across her face.

Chapter Seventeen

Annie's day had been quite a nightmare. It was her birthday, and she had been forced to attend a surprise party that had been thrown by André. The only problem was, her brother could not keep a secret to save his life. She had known about the party within the first few hours after he had started planning it. She had forced Gary into confession, and he had given her all the facts. She had, of course, sworn him to secrecy, and had feigned surprise when everyone leapt out at her.

She had managed to stay in a corner for most of the afternoon, watching everyone else. She was on the brink of confirming the rumours that were flying about. The rumours said that Ali Rice was seeing Harley, and from the way they acted at the party, she was pretty sure it was true. Even so, André had bullied her into accepting a second date with him, for the following afternoon. She had already made arrangements to meet Barry at a swim meet he had been called about, before they all went to the Bouvais house for Sunday lunch. Then Harley was to come and pick her up, to make up for the previous date. She'd had to endure the wrath of both Carlene and her brother to the point where it had been impossible not to accept in the end.

The problem was, he seemed to be harmless. She had no rational explanation for why she did not want to see him. She couldn't simply say 'I can't go out with Harley because he reminds me of a guy I don't like in my dreams'. It would sound stupid to anyone who didn't know about the dreams. All she could tell for definite was that he could not to be trusted, although she could no sooner say why than she could tell Matthew Wilkins why she needed to be close to him.

Annie had finally managed to escape the party at 8pm, leaving most people still partying heartily. At last, she was alone with her thoughts. Joanna had gone home after a family emergency, and the girl who had originally shared their suite of rooms had moved out to live with her boyfriend, leaving Annie totally alone. There was no one to see her lie awake at night. Not that she could have slept anyway, because what had started as a light rain at 9:30 had turned into a full storm by midnight. She sat on her bed, and watched as the rain made patterns on the window. Lightning lashed across the sky soundlessly. Out side, a lone figure was walking under a bright orange umbrella, and Annie envied their ability to be lost within the storm. A few minutes later, another figure appeared, moving away from the dorm house toward the bridge. Annie watched, thinking for a moment that it might be

Matthew, but realising even as she thought it that it was wishful thinking. There was no way he was out on a night like that. But watching the figure, she imagined that it *was* him, that he had been on the brink of coming to her.

If it hadn't been for the storm, though, she probably would have slept. She had discovered that she could keep herself from dreaming if she didn't sleep for too long. After Matthew had last been there, she had taken his advice, and managed to sleep. She had woken up two hours later, feeling more relaxed than she had for a long while. Now she had taken to setting her alarm to wake her every couple of hours. Better still, though, the fact that Joanna was away meant that she did not disturb anyone if she *did* start to dream rather loudly.

She could not bring herself to sleep until the storm was over, anyway. When she was younger, she had been afraid of the storm, but she was older now. She was finally out of her teens. It was a long time since she had been a little girl. For her sixth birthday, Annie's father had given her a plastic horse, promising that it would one day be replaced by a real one. It had never come, though. The plastic horse was still around, hidden away in a large box full of Barbie dolls. It was missing an ear; it had broken off on a trip to Tulsa to stay with her grandparents. The fine mane of silvery hair had unfortunately been washed, after André's action man went for fireman training, and had never been quite the same since. It was one of the few things she would keep eternally. It was the last birthday gift he had ever given her. He died a few days before she turned seven.

Thirteen further years of life had changed the world in which she lived, and changed the life she had been given. All of the most important events had happened to her since then. Her first date, the day the braces went on, and came off, her first violin recital, the accident that had ruined her left hand. Even now it was possible to see the damage done by the accident that had ruined her chances of fame and glory with her violin. It had damaged all the cartilage in her wrist, letting it waste away until the fluidity was almost completely gone, and she put her violin days behind her. Her graduation, the photograph of her and André in their graduation robes still stood on the piano that her father had loved so much, had been a sentimental day without him there.

"Oh, daddy, I wish you were here. You'd know what to do. And you would love Matthew. He's the one. I wish you could meet him." She cried softly. As if in answer, a huge rumble of thunder filled the air.

Sitting by the window wasn't helping her nerves any, so she stood and made her way into the living room, flicking on the TV before moving into the kitchen. She made her hot chocolate in a pan on the stove, stirring until it was smooth and hot, then poured it into her favourite mug. In the ice box, there was a half full carton of pecan fudge swirl ice cream, temptingly soft, and calling out to her. If it weren't for the fact that she was hardly eating anything at the moment, she would have ignored the call of it. Her lack of nutrition was becoming apparent around her face, and in her wrist where the ruined cartilage showed more than ever.

The soft, sticky ice cream was very welcome in her stomach, and once started, Annie found it hard to stop. The hot liquid in the mug steamed on the coffee table in front of her as she flicked through the channels. Finally, she found Amazing Discoveries.

"So, what do we get for the price?" The presenter was asking. This was Annie's favourite part, where the presenter kept asking for more merchandise for an 'amazingly low price', and the other person would give in, supplying not one but two bottles of amazing tooth whitener, or whatever it was they happened to be selling. Today was the turn of a super mop which was claiming to be 100% drip less, and at only $39.95 including 3 extra mop heads and a bucket, which would normally sell alone for $49.95 in the stores. Annie couldn't help but laugh, until seven minutes and 29 seconds past one, when the electricity cut out, and the only light was coming from the storm outside.

Chapter Eighteen

There was nothing like a rainy night when he managed to get laid, Harley thought to himself. Ali lay in his double bed, sleeping soundly, refreshing herself for later. Out on the fire escape, Harley breathed in the night air, warm and wet, filled with electricity. He couldn't help but marvel at the fork lightning in the sky above him, and the fact that there were probably very few others watching it. There were no other people out at 3 o'clock in the morning, so sitting where he was, he was not bothered by his own nakedness.

There was wine in the glass in his hand, full and red, almost like blood, as Ali had commented as she pulled the cork from the bottle and poured it. He took a mouthful, and toasted the woman in bed. The light of a dozen candles flickered across the surface of her skin, smooth and tanned as it was. She may not be the most beautiful creature in the world, but she did have talent.

He had managed to get himself another date with Annie for later that day. He was already trying to figure out exactly what he could do to get back at her. Of course, it wasn't just her, but that teacher guy, as well. The rain might mean he had to be a little more careful, but he would take his chances. She would not get away with it. His other intention was to make Ali jealous, to tease her like she had teased him all afternoon, hanging all over that guy, Barry, who was apparently a super jock of the swimming pool. The tease had had the desired effect, and when they finally found themselves alone together, their passions had exploded over and over again.

He had left the party first, a little before 11pm. It had already been raining fairly hard, but he had waited for her. He had watched and waited as a few other people left, and eventually, she appeared. At some point, she had managed to change her clothes, and he wondered if she kept clothes there for occasions when she had stayed with Barry.

"Are we going back to yours, or would you like to come to mine?" She asked when she reached him.

"Mine." He replied. But he couldn't wait for that long. Luckily, she had changed out of the ridiculous pants she had been wearing, into a skirt, so it wasn't difficult for him to do anything when he pinned her to a tree round the back of the frat house. The rain had been warm as she allowed him to do the job, rolling down his back through the thin shirt he had been wearing. When they finally reached the motel room, they had stripped unashamedly in front of each other, and went straight to bed, before finally collapsing into a heap several hours later. She had a way of making him feel good that he had never had with a girl before.

Now, he sat on the wooden steps at the back of the chalet, which formed a fire escape down to the ground only a few feet away, smoking his cigarette, drinking his wine. He loved to be completely undressed, as he was now, with the rain falling over him. He had never had the opportunity to do that back home.

Harley had grown up in Seattle, with Carlene. Originally, they had lived with their parents. Then there was an accident, when Harley was fifteen, and Carlene was almost seventeen. It had been a disaster of epic proportions, which left their mother unable to move, and their father in a grave. They had then been sent to live with their grandparents, who had been rather restrictive on them. Carlene had moved out to go to college about a year later, leaving Harley alone with them. If it hadn't been for a couple of the girls in his class, he would have gone completely mad. But they had done good jobs, and it was due to them that he now knew what he was doing with Ali.

Three years had passed slowly, and they eventually took their toll. One day, his grandparents got a call from the hospital where his mother had been living for the past two years. She had slipped away peacefully in the night, or so they said. Harley didn't believe it, though. When both grandparents died within a couple of weeks of each other, very recently as it happened, Harley had made the decision to move closer to his sister. She was all he had left now. And the best part was, he had managed to hook up with a girl already. One that didn't seem to mind what he was.

Eventually, he knew he was going to have to

choose a course and enrol in classes, but he couldn't do that until the start of the next semester. Until then, he was just happy to hang out in his motel room. He had some cash, now. He and Carlene had done okay out of their losses. The family house had been sold a long time ago, but the money had gone into trust for them. Their parents had taken out the best medical insurance possible, and it had been plenty to keep their mother comfortable for the rest of her days. Now that he was nineteen, he had more money than most kids his age, so did Carlene for that matter. Eventually, he would invest in some property, but for now, the motel would do.

There was nothing he could do about his past, now, but there was plenty he could do about the future. He had a few plans in mind already, plans that would see him retain his power and status for a lot longer than most kids could imagine. His first step was to get back his dignity, and make the girl in the bed his and his alone. He would work on the rest as it came to him.

There was a change in Ali's breathing. It was something he had learned a long time ago, the way breathing changes when the body wakes naturally, quickening gently until the body has enough oxygen to support conscious thought. Right now, Ali was stirring, and he had to admit that the change in her breath brought about a change in him. He took another mouthful of wine, and smiled to himself.

"I hope you slept well." He said, without turning to look at her.

"Very." She replied. He could feel her eyes on his back, and listened to her sitting up, letting the sheet fall to the floor with a gentle swish of fabric. "Are you coming back here, or do I have to come get you?"

"Come get me, baby, cause I think I need a little of you right here." He replied, turning to her, pointing at his groin, and waiting for her to come. She slid off the bed, and moved across to where he sat. He moved slightly so that she could sit in his lap, and together they watched the storm rage on.

Chapter Nineteen

My brother's joining was followed by all the festivities that usually took place. Alim and Kylin stood together in the sun, and I stood by their side, with Haltar. As I walked away from them, Grey took my arm and led me away further.

"Anicia, you were correct. Alim was called to the council by your father last night, and they have confirmed that the quake is to come soon, maybe within the few days that follow from now. They have vowed that we will leave on the seventh night from now. There is no way that there will now be time for you to be joined to Haltar. I believe that had you not been in the isolation chamber last night, that you may well have been joined to him this day, but our customs forbid the joining of someone who has been in isolation for the night before.

There is no time for the ceremony to be arranged now. I now have hope that you shall be bringing Alina with us?" Grey told me, his voice filled with anxiety.

"I encourage your persistence, my friend, and if I may have my love, then you too may have yours. Now, I must ask for you to excuse me, for I must speak with Brace on urgent business." I spoke as quickly as he, then continued on to Brace, where he stood shocked and stung by some words that Alexis had uttered. "Brace, may we speak?"

"Of course. What worries you, my friend?" Brace asked.

"It was this night just passed, while I was locked into the isolation chamber, my senses heightened by the surrounding darkness, within the very centre of the night. When sleep was almost upon me, I was suddenly alerted to the sound of voices not far away. The voices spoke of love, love shared between the two...." I paused, embarrassed by the words I was about to speak. "It is little more than a physical love, but the act has already occurred. I think that more of an emotional love is growing between the two."

"Why do you tell me of this?" Brace demanded.

"Because, my friend, the voices belonged to Alexis and Haltar."

Chapter Twenty

Barry's head was pounding. The party hadn't been that good, he thought. But here he was, lying in bed, with a hangover - and a person. It wasn't Ali, though. He could tell that instantly. Firstly, the body shape was all wrong, secondly, there was red hair spread right across his own pillow. It could only be one person, Libby Fisher.

He sat up quickly, making his head spin rather too much, and tried to remember the chain of events that led him to being in bed with his girlfriend's roommate. He had absolutely no idea, but still, here he was. Then he realised that although they must have slept in the same bed, nothing could have happened, because they were both fully clothed. Besides, he knew far too much to ever believe that a girl like Libby Fisher would allow herself to be bedded by the likes of him.

It wasn't through a lack of willing on his part,

though. He had tried, he just hadn't been terribly productive in his attempts. He had spent a great deal of his early years swimming, becoming all state champion when he was still in junior high. That was how he managed to meet Annie and André Bouvais. He had been taking part in a swim meet, when he was about fourteen, and Annie had greeted him instantly as if he were an old friend. Annie had drawn him instantly into her group of friends, and she had done it with such ferocity that he had not even stopped to ask her why. Before that time, he'd had so few friends outside of swimming that his parents had started to wonder if he might be troubled in some way. The twins put an end to that worry, as he became friends with both them, and their friend Gary Hutchins.

Years had passed, and the group of friends became closer through out them. Finally, they had all started college together. Barry's parents had wanted him to go to college in California, where they had heard about some programme that would help him to the Olympics, but Barry had been stubborn, and had not allowed them to talk him into it. Besides, the college he *was* attending, had a perfectly good swim team that would give him all the training he really needed. Plus, they gave him a full scholarship, which hadn't even been an option in California. And then, within a few days of starting college, he was dating Ali Rice. Annie couldn't stand her, and on more than one occasion had warned him that she would break his heart. He had to wonder now how she had known.

In those days, she had really seemed to like him. They had done all the things that couples usually did with each other. Eventually, they were going steady, or so he assumed. Most of the time, it turned out he was wrong. Yet now, here he was, in his own bed, with Libby Fisher spread out beside him.

"Libby?" He asked as he gently shook her arm, which was clad in a pale violet angora sleeve that would have looked better on a brunette. "Libby, wake up."

"Oh, I'm sorry, sugar." She smiled sleepily as she turned to look at him. She pulled her arms out from under the covers, revealing that they were tied together with a pair of his own tube socks. "Help a poor girl out, won't you, huh?"

"This may be a ridiculous question, Libby, but what exactly are you doing here, in my bed?" Barry asked, trying to untie the tube socks which she had offered up to him. "And who tied you up?"

"D'you always get forgetful when you been drinkin'? You tied me up, sugar. And you offered to do a whole lot more, too. Then you fell asleep, leavin' me all tied up with no place to go." Libby smiled again. Barry had always been led to believe that southern girls had a certain amount of class. Libby was running a little short of that amount right then.

"What about Ali?" He asked, a little confused.

"Well, she made her exit a little early, with that nice young man, Harley. Then you and I started havin' a little fun for ourselves. Mind you, I did hope you might get a little further south, if you get what I mean, sugar. I always heard you had a little talent in that area." She replied.

"Harley? Carlene's brother? Well, that figures, doesn't it? Don't tell me, he's the latest guy she's been seeing behind my back. Nothing changes, does it? I thought she was finally getting settled with me. I've spent all this time with her, and nothing is changing. Damn that girl, I've had it with her!" Barry sighed. It was definitely not the first time she had been caught cheating on him. They had, after all, been dating each other for almost two years now. She had a knack of flirting with just about every male she ever came across, regardless of who they may be. He had watched her at it, far too many times for him to keep count anymore. He had even had to watch her as she tried to get her hooks into the anthropology teacher when he had first arrived. Luckily, the teacher *really* wasn't interested in Ali, because if she had managed to get her claws in, she never would have let *him* go.

"You said you were goin' to teach him a lesson, but I'm guessin' you forgot that bit, too. Well, never mind, cause we can make up for lost time later. I've been thinkin' for a while you really deserve far better than her." Libby told him, her voice thick with such sweetness that he thought she may well give herself cavities. She climbed off the bed, revealing the shortest skirt he had ever seen, and the creamiest thighs within it. He watched her stretch her arms above her head, revealing an inch of her smooth, flat stomach. He wondered again how he had managed to end up in bed with Libby, and how he had managed to forget every moment of it. When she leaned across the bed toward him and kissed him hard on the lips, he thought he was probably going to faint. "You call me, sugar, and we can have a real good time, one even Ali would be jealous of, hmm?"

"Uh, okay, sure." He grinned as she sashayed out of the room, her red hair swinging loose around her shoulders. As she pulled the door closed behind her, he fell back on the pillows, fighting the urge to run after her and drag her back to bed caveman style. He lay there, trying to remember exactly how he had managed to get her back to his room, but all he could remember was Annie and André telling him to go easy on the beer because he had a swim meet the next day.

He clapped his hand to his forehead as he remembered the swim meet he was supposed to be going to. Glancing at his wristwatch, he realised he had less than fifteen minutes to get across campus to the pool. He didn't even stop long enough to shave, although he did brush his teeth, as he rushed out of the door of the frat house where he and his friends had ruled the roost since they had arrived.

He grabbed his bike from the shed at the back of the house, and cycled as quickly as his headache would allow him to. He knew that as soon as he hit the water, the pain would dispel entirely. He made it to the pool with a few minutes to spare, and chained his bike to the rack at the front. Then he realised that the place was deserted.

As usual, the door was unlocked. Barry made his way into the locker room, and started to change out of his clothes. It wasn't unusual for the times of meets to be changed at short notice, but as he had only been called about the meet the day before, he found it hard to believe that it had been changed all ready. He hadn't even taken the call himself. One of the year's new pledges had taken it, and told him about it a few hours later. Maybe the kid had got the time wrong. It was possible, of course. He had just taken for granted that the information would be accurate.

He had suggested that Annie and André come to watch him swim. Then they would all go back to the

Bouvais house for Sunday lunch. Mrs. Bouvais had taken pity on Barry, a couple of years earlier, when his parents had left for California, where, after all, there was more to do than swimming. They had hoped that he would go with them, but by then, he had no desire to leave the town where he had grown up. The fact was, he felt more at home with the twins than he had ever felt with his own parents, and all he wanted was for his friendship with them to last forever. Their mother had almost adopted him after that, fussing over him as if he was one of her own. He often got the feeling she would have rather liked more children, and that she would have had them if Mr. Bouvais had not died.

As Barry dove into the water, he felt his head start to clear. He warmed up first, swimming gently back and forth. Then he started to swim faster and harder, knowing that the only way he would ever make the Olympics was to train for them. Swimming gave him a chance to think, also. So what if Ali was cheating on him again, he thought. It wasn't the first time. But it would be the last, he decided. As soon as he was done there, he would call her and tell her as much. He was tired of the games she always felt the need to play. She had made a fool of him for the very last time. As he swam faster and faster, his head became so clear, that he was left to wonder what he had even been thinking about.

In fact, Barry was so busy swimming that he didn't hear the door opening, or the sound of street shoes on the poolside. He didn't notice there was a stranger in the pool area until he reached the side. He was about to tell the guy to get out when his head started to crack again, as a hard object made contact with it, and everything went dark.

Chapter Twenty-one

It was amazing how fresh everything seemed after the night of down pours. The storm had not kept Matthew awake like he knew it had Annie. He had merely been content to watch the light in her dorm room window. When the power went out, he watched as a candle was lit, and flickered for hours until finally burning itself out. Not until then did he finally allow himself to sleep for a couple of hours. Once again, shortly after dawn, he pulled himself from the bed to watch her running. She seemed to look happier than she had done a few days earlier. On some level, he hoped he had helped her by holding her so tightly when she had asked him to.

After that, he tried to get an early start on grading some test papers he had been avoiding since Friday. He was about halfway through reading the paper of some kid named Humphrey Briggs when he started to dose off. When he finally woke up again, it was 11:45, and there was no way he could go back to the papers until he cleared his head a little.

He found himself wandering around aimlessly for a while. He thought about heading for the coffee house, but it was Sunday, so it was closed until 2. His next idea was to go and watch the guys playing football on the field, but he found he couldn't get enthusiastic enough for that. In the end, he found himself wandering around down by the river. He was halfway across the bridge when he came face to face with Annie.

"Hi!" She smiled brightly.

"Hey, Annie, How are you doing?" He asked.

"Much better, thanks. I'm on my way to watch Barry Oakland swimming. He's all state champion, you know." She replied. He hadn't realised that Barry was the athletic type. He didn't seem it. "I think it sounds more impressive than it actually is. Would you mind walking with me a while? I hate this walk on my own."

"I know what you mean. That bit just by the pool is about as charming as the Black hole of Calcutta!" He agreed, and was surprised at the ease with which he fell in to step beside her. "At least you don't look tired any more. I'll take it you're sleeping a little better than you were?"

"Yes, and eating, too. Well, that is, I've been eating if pecan fudge swirl ice cream at midnight counts." She replied, and he laughed.

"It counts if it's the only thing. I think the nurse recommended proper food, though. I recommend fish stick sandwiches, with ketchup. I know, it sounds revolting, but it's really not so bad."

"I take it you're a fish stick fan?"

"Well, they're quick, and easy, and rather good between two slices of bread. Those chicken fingers aren't bad, either."

"You need food supervision."

"I do not. I eat very well, if you must know. I just don't have much time anymore. I have a stack of papers at home waiting to be graded before Wednesday, and I've only managed three of them so far. At present, I happen to be doing a very fine job of procrastinating, if you must know."

"That's a nice, big word. So, am I keeping you from your procrastination?"

"No, actually, you are doing a very good job of helping me with it, thanks."

They made their way toward the pool, but he walked as slowly as he could, knowing that when they got there, he would have to leave her. She seemed so much brighter than she had the last time he had seen her. He hoped that she really was sleeping better. He didn't like the idea of her lying awake in the spare room at his parents' house all weekend. Even so, he knew that the thought of the weekend that was now fast approaching had to be helping her to feel more at ease.

They walked slowly through a group of trees, and then were faced with the least pleasant area on campus. The ground was like a wasteland, covered in empty beer cans and discarded condoms. Right in the centre, there was a scorched ring of earth where fires were built to keep kids warm as they drank and fornicated beneath the stars. Matthew had first seen it about a week into his first semester of teaching, when he had observed a group of kids there. He had done his best to look the other way;

after all, it wasn't so long since he had been a student himself. In fact, in so many ways, he still was one.

"A few of the guys came here after the party yesterday." Annie told him, sounding a little disgusted by them.

"Did you have fun?" He asked,

"Well, the party was supposed to be for me, but to be honest, I wasn't really all that impressed. I left at 8pm, and I believe that everyone else had a much better time than I did. I was bullied rather mercilessly by my brother into going out with that guy Harley again, which I am *not* impressed with, because I really didn't want to see him ever again. If only there was some way of convincing him that I'm not interested. Actually, the whole party was just a glorified excuse for André to get people to like him more." She replied.

"Do you even like your brother?" He joked. She stopped and looked at him, her green eyes seeming to process the question.

"Lets put it this way." She replied at last. "I love him, but most of the time, I can't stand him. He's a jerk sometimes, and he seems to think the world revolves around him. I mean, take that ridiculous squiggle above the 'e' in his name. He added that himself when he was nine because he thought it was so much more impressive for crying out loud! I wish I didn't feel that way about him, but really, he bugs me sometimes."

"You'd miss him if he weren't there, though." He told her.

"I know I would, and I can't imagine my life without him. We're twins, for crying out loud, we're linked to each other. It doesn't mean I have to like him, though." She admitted. He knew exactly what she meant. "Come on, we shouldn't hang around here too long. Who knows when the stoners will get here today? I have to wonder, do you think they go to church or something."

"No." He chuckled. "They stay in bed until 3pm, then wonder why they haven't managed to do their home work."

"How would you know whether they did it or not? After all, you're avoiding grading them."

"Ha, ha. Actually, most of the time, I don't mind grading papers. The problem is, I keep having to refer to those lesson plans I keep getting given, because the stuff I'm teaching is so far from accurate that I have to check that I'm grading in line with what I taught. If I find out who ran to Professor Mitchell, I'll do them some damage. Actually, I have no idea how to do people damage, so I'll probably just give them evil looks for the next month."

"Evil looks? I don't believe that you're capable of evil looks. But if you are, maybe you could teach me, because other wise I think I may get stuck with Harley."

"That won't happen."

"It might just. I might just have to hide every time he appears. I might just have to avoid leaving my dorm room ever again."

"If he gets too clingy, just tell him. You have a certain amount of power, if you ask me. I mean, look at the way you have managed to live with the dreams for all this time. That takes energy. I very much doubt that there is any weakness in you."

"It's nice of you to say, but I'm not sure it's true. Oh, look, we made it."

They were suddenly in front of the pool. Something didn't seem quite right, though. He had expected there to be many more people around. There was only one bike in the rack, and no one else to be seen. Annie looked a little worried, too.

"I'm sure there's nothing wrong." He said, doubting his own words. She looked at him, worry in her eyes, before turning, and started to run into the pool building. He started to run behind her, realising that there *must* be something wrong. When he got to the poolside, Annie was already in the pool, trying to pull her friend from the water.

"Help me." She cried. Within seconds, he was also in the water, and together they hauled him out.

Chapter Twenty-two

Annie never made her appointment with Harley. She never made it home for Sunday lunch. Instead, she spent most of the afternoon at the hospital, waiting for news. The doctors were running tests. They had done a brain scan, and blood tests, hoping to make sure that there would be no lasting damage. In the end, they decided he was not in any imminent danger, but that they would keep him in overnight for observation.

Luckily, they had arrived at the pool within a couple of minutes of him being injured. There was no way of telling how things would have turned out if they had not been there. The reality of it made her blood run cold, knowing that someone had purposefully hurt him. And she couldn't help but be thankful that Matthew had been with her. There was no way she could have lifted

Barry from the water by herself. Matthew knew CPR, and had worked on getting Barry to breathe while she called the paramedics. By the time they arrived, Barry was breathing by himself, but still very drowsy.

She had gone with Barry, while Matthew stayed behind, talking to campus security, knowing that someone had attacked Barry. They were going to look at the surveillance tapes to see if they could identify the attacker, but Annie got the feeling they were not going to be so lucky. He had promised he would make his way to the hospital later to make sure that Barry was all right.

Now, Annie was waiting patiently to see Barry. Despite the fact that he didn't seem to be affected by his injuries, the doctor had insisted that they not over crowd the room and that his visitors be kept to a minimum. At the moment, Gary and André were in with him, while she waited out side. She hadn't even had a chance to find out what was going on.

The most surprising thing was that Ali actually managed to breeze in and out of the hospital. Annie wondered if it may be that she was feeling a little guilty about her actions in the recent past. She had said that she couldn't stay long, because she had somewhere she had to be. Annie was simply surprised she had managed to turn up at all. According to Gary, she had left the party just before he had left to make his way to the coffee house, and when he got outside, he had spotted Ali making her way round the back of the house with Harley. Annie knew it was only a matter of time now before the rumours were confirmed.

Finally, Annie managed to get into the room. The nurse had left her station to check on some other patient, and Annie slipped through the door unnoticed. The three guys seemed to be laughing at something, and she looked on them all with the affection of a sister.

"Hey, Annie, get yourself over here." Barry grinned when he noticed her. "This girl saved my life, you know. She is my new superhero."

"I did have help, you know." She told them quietly, realising once more how bad it would look that she had been walking alone with Matthew.

"We know that." Gary smiled at her, wrapping his arm around her shoulders, and whispering in her ear. "They have no idea."

"Well, as the hero of the day, I think you deserve another party!" Barry said, still smiling from ear to ear.

"There will be no more partying for any of you, at least not for the moment." She responded sharply, wondering if it wasn't the party that had got him into this trouble in the first place. "Guys, d'you think I could have just a minute with Barry, by myself?"

"Sure." The other two replied together. They left the room, and she was alone with her friend.

"What happened?" She asked him, moving closer to the bed.

"I have no idea, Annie. I was swimming; I didn't even notice the guy come in until he was right next to me. He was wearing a hood, so I couldn't even see his face. I was going to tell him to get lost, because he was wearing street shoes, but then it all went dark, so I didn't get the chance." He told her. "I can't believe I let it happen."

"I don't think you were in any position to fight back. Can you think of anyone who would want to do this to you?" She asked, already having an idea of her own, but unwilling to voice it first.

"None. Maybe I offended someone. Maybe it was

random. I really can't say." He replied. She got the feeling he might still be kidding himself about the situation. "I do know that you were right about something, though."

"What's that, sweetie?"

"About Ali. You remember you warned me about her, once. You told me that she was going to break my heart. I should have known, I guess. When I woke up next to Libby Fisher this morning, she told me the truth. She told me that Ali was sleeping with Harley. Sorry I have to break the news to you." He revealed. She didn't have the heart to tell him she already knew the truth.

"I'm sorry, Barry." She sighed, sitting down in the plastic chair beside the bed. "You deserve better than Alison Rice, Barry, you always have. I'm not sure that Libby Fisher is a better choice, but at least I like her, in a funny way."

"I don't think I'm going to start seeing Libby, and for what it's worth, nothing happened between us. I just wish I hadn't wasted so long with Ali."

"Sometimes we have to waste our time to get to where we are supposed to be." Annie assured him. The noise of the door opening drew her attention away from Barry. She turned and saw Matthew at the door, and waved him to come over. "Any more information, yet?"

"None, I'm afraid. How are you, Barry?" He asked, seeming genuinely interested.

"Good, thanks. And thanks for helping Annie save me. I don't think I was quite ready to die yet." Barry answered.

"I'm glad." Matthew admitted, seeming relieved. When the door swung open again, they both looked. This time, it was the nurse who had come to check how he was doing.

"Okay, everyone out, now." She announced, and Annie felt annoyed that she had not managed to tell her friend more before she was expelled. She leant over the bed, kissed him on the top of the head, and told him she would see him later. Together, they made their way back out into the hallway. Gary and André seemed to be having a discussion about something, and so neither of them was watching as Annie and Matthew walked off down the corridor chatting.

"He has no idea what happened." Annie sighed. She hadn't felt so helpless in a very long time. "So, is there really no information?"

"That isn't exactly the case, no." He confessed. "Come on, I'll buy you a coffee."

They made their way into the coffee shop that was across the building. Annie was starting to get a little concerned, now. If Matthew knew something, why hadn't he told Barry? Why was he not telling her? He bought a couple of coffees, and they made their way into the seating area. Finally sitting opposite each other, she could tell it must be bad.

"Spill it." She demanded.

"Well," he started. She got the feeling he didn't know exactly where to start. "There were pictures on the tape. The problem is, they were fuzzed. I don't know how, but the attacker was fuzzed while the rest of the picture was fine. They even called the AV squad, and they can't figure it out. The pictures clearly show Barry going in. About ten minutes later, the attacker goes in, then out a minute later. You run in about two minutes after the attacker goes out. Whoever it was, they were there just before us. They think he must have been fairly athletic, just from the shape and size of him........"

"I already know what you're thinking. How do I tell Barry that the guy who stole his girlfriend just tried to smash his head in?" Annie questioned.

"I don't know, Annie. I can tell you that looking at those tapes, there is a distinct similarity to him." He confirmed. They both fell silent. She wasn't sure what else to say, so she decided it was probably best not to say anything at all. They sat in silence for almost three minutes before he spoke again. "I'm sorry if your weekend wasn't all you had hoped, Annie."

"Well, it wasn't that bad. I do wish I hadn't got older, but that's life. Hell, I have to grow up sometime, I guess."

"You aren't old."

"That's what I thought Friday. I don't know, birthdays take it out of me. How are you supposed to be thrilled by getting older? Sure, when I was twelve, I liked the presents and everything, but it seems like a bit of a chore now. Like Christmas."

"Christmas isn't a chore. I'm not so keen on New Year, but that has more to do with the fact that when it turned midnight when I was a kid, I always had to put up with my mom kissing me on the cheek, telling me off for not being at a party with some girl or other." He confided, his face looking slightly flushed, she realised. "Besides, twenty isn't old. You have all the time in the world to find out who you are."

"Yeah, but I am starting to question why I picked the major that I did, and exactly what use anthropology is supposed to be to me. Sorry, I know it's your passion, and I love it as a subject, but really, what am I going to do with it?"

"I'm not sure. I knew when I started the subject that I was going to teach it. But anthropology isn't your major, is it. Think about it, for a minute or two, why *did* you choose to study any of your subjects?"

"Well, I chose American history and forensic psychology for some reason. I think there was a guidance counsellor who told me that I would need those subjects if I wanted to work as a certain type of historian, which I think I did at the time. Anthropology just seemed to fit in with that."

"So, forensic psychology would help you if you were interested in solving mysteries, and the American history would help you understand the history surrounding them, possibly. Actually, anthropology, forensic psychology and archaeology would be the better combination, although that would become your major, I guess. Or do you want to write about them? If that was the case, then your courses are right. Besides, there is a problem with the archaeology programme here, because Professor Mitchell teaches it, and I know how out of date his understanding is. Worryingly so, if you ask me."

"You know, I haven't even thought about the future for a couple years, now. Not since I left high school."

"Is that not because you are too caught up in the past?"

"Possibly."

"Possibly what?" Asked a voice from beside her. She hadn't even noticed the tall blond male as he arrived. She had been dreading the point where she would have to speak to Harley again, knowing that it would be hard for her to be civil to the person she believed had something to do with Barry's head being cracked. "Your brother didn't know where you had gone to, so I told him I'd track you down, and here you are. I was wondering if we might be able to continue with our plans for the afternoon now that your friend isn't in any danger any more."

"I really don't think I can leave the hospital. Barry might need something. I want to be close by in case he does." She told him, not willing to admit that she just didn't want to go out with him.

"But you left him to come here with this guy." Harley pointed out.

"Well, that's my fault." Matthew volunteered. "I dragged Annie away for a tutorial. We were supposed to meet to discuss Annie's options for later career opportunities. I have a contact at the New Mexico state museum, and I was trying to arrange some kind of internship for her."

"And that couldn't wait?" Harley spat.

"No, unfortunately. Next weekend, they are holding interviews for the position, so I was briefing Annie on the job specifics." Matthew lied. Annie was rather amazed at the speed with which he offered the information.

"You mean to tell me that this guy is going to get you this job? What does he expect in return?" Harley's voice was so full of malice that Annie had to wonder exactly what he thought was going on between them.

"I'm not sure that's any of your business." Annie told him. "But I don't intend to give any kind of service for it. What do you take me for?"

"It's what I take him for." Harley inferred.

"As she said, it's none of your business." Matthew told him, standing up. "If you really must know, then I should tell you right now that neither you nor I are ever going to go there with this girl. Annie is a wonderful girl, but she needs something that you are not. She needs her match, the one person who is out there just for her. You are not that person, I'm afraid."

"You're trying to sell that fate crap to the wrong person." Harley yelled. "Do you think that anyone is stupid enough to believe in 'soul mates'? You pricks all think that because you have a little information that you can tell the world what to think. I hate guys like you."

"Think what you like." Matthew yelled back. "Annie and I are pupil and teacher, nothing more than that. Don't blame the fact that you couldn't get her into bed on your first date on me. This girl may be the nicest I have ever known, but that is as far as it goes. And for the record, she deserves a hell of a lot better than you. If you aren't bright enough to understand that, then maybe you really shouldn't be here at all."

"Hey, that's rich coming from the guy who believes in fate. How the hell do you expect anyone to believe that crap? There is no such thing as a soul, and I promise you, there is no such thing as reincarnation. That one is an even bigger joke! Soul mates, for Christ's sake, how can you expect anyone to believe it's true? Other than anything else, true love doesn't exist." Harley laughed nastily.

"Yes it does." Her voice was so quiet that they barely even realised that she had spoken, but they both turned to look at her. She could feel the tears stinging her eyes "Fate exists, true love exists. The soul is a more immense thing than you will ever understand, and I have proof of that."

The tears were spilling down her cheeks now. She could feel them, warm and damp, flowing freely. She was sure that her words were the truth. She looked at Matthew, and his expression told her he understood. Harley, however, started to laugh. The rage inside of her began to grow, pulsating through her veins. Finally, it burst forth in a thundering motion that lunged at Harley, ripping trenches into his face, bringing his own, thick blood bubbling to the surface.

"Bitch!" Harley screamed, and covered his cheek with his hand. With the other hand, he grabbed Annie's arm, and twisted it around behind her back before Matthew had a chance to fight him off. Annie stood frozen, her head held back now by Harley's spare hand. A trickle of his blood dropped onto her skin, and she felt herself go rigid. Matthew's hands were suddenly upon Harley, and he finally let Annie free. She fell to the ground, and watched as Harley and Matthew fought.

"Hey, you kids, take it outside!" The old lady at the cash register finally interjected. But it did not work, and Annie was left to look on as Matthew hit Harley in the face, and Harley broke Matthew's arm.

Chapter Twenty-three

The pain was excruciating. Matthew had never had a broken bone before, so this one was a good start. His whole wrist was limp, swelling larger and larger by the minute. Annie had helped him down to the emergency room, where they had taken x-rays, and put a cast round it.

"I guess this means you'll have to do the driving next weekend." Matthew grinned as his wrist was being wrapped.

"You're crazy! Harley could've killed you. I told you he wasn't a good guy." Annie wasn't smiling. *So she cares just a little bit then*, he thought, but the smile faded from his face all the same.

"Yeah, after he'd killed you." He stated soberly.

"I know." Annie acknowledged, then added in a

lighter tone "I gave him a nice scar, though, didn't I! Look, I still have his skin under my finger nails."

"That was good, but honestly, you need to be careful." He told her, and watched *her* smile fading. The nurse finished his cast, and left them alone at last. "If he really was the one who hurt Barry, then I don't think that there is much we are going to be able to do to get him off our case. We could call the cops, I guess, but what kind of evidence do we have? The blurred video isn't going to prove our story."

"Exactly, and what would the motive have been? Maybe he wants Ali all to himself, but that isn't reason to do someone in. He has Ali, he's been sleeping with Ali, since that night in the coffee house, the night *I* went out with him, so how can he think that this will get him something better?" She vented her frustration at the room. "I'm sorry, it's just that he scares me, Matthew. The whole day has been filled with me doing things I really shouldn't be doing, because there are all these rules, and I can't get past them. Then I nearly get my neck snapped, and you get your wrist shattered into tiny pieces, and if that weren't bad enough, the whole coffee shop will have noticed that I was there with you. If I get you fired, you have full authority to get me expelled, okay?"

"We did have that discussion, didn't we? Annie, it doesn't make any difference. You and I were discussing the welfare of another pupil, and then we discussed your future career prospects. Nothing that we discussed this afternoon is against any rules. And to be honest, I don't think that there are really any rules against any of this."

"Maybe if you just made this kind of effort with

the other students." Annie suggested. He knew what she meant, because the treatment he was giving her seemed so

"I am *trying* to get to know everyone in my classes." He assured her. "The problem is, I memorise by row, from back to front, so to be honest, other than Ali, I don't know the names of a single person in the front three rows yet. You, being at the back all the time, I memorised your name in the first wave. Like that girl, Bonnie, the one who sits across the aisle from you, or Evan Sanders who sits two seats over, one row forward. I *am* working on it. And just because I happen to have socialised with you, doesn't mean I'm giving you better grades or anything."

"I still think I should try to keep a low profile around campus for a while. I prefer when no one notices me. I never wanted to stand out, so I think, for a while, I'll keep myself to myself, and avoid going out in public."

"I doubt you can blend in that well. Don't hide from anything." He looked at her, finding it hard to believe he could have been selfish enough to worry about being close to her when she was scared she might be disciplined for socialising with him. If she knew the truth of his thoughts, she would surely worry even further. He had barely even admitted to himself yet that he had made a mistake with education, and that he was only staying because of her. "You know, when I was at college, before I was sent here, we used to socialise with all the professors. I remember one time when a whole group of us went to this house party thrown by one of them. We thought nothing of it. The rules aren't that strict, you know. They're flexible."

"The other good thing about hiding, though, is

that I wouldn't have to worry about running in to Harley. I can't help it, he scares me too much, Matthew." She told him, brushing her dark hair out of her green eyes, and tucking it behind her ears. She really did look scared, and there was not hint of a smile on her face now. He could feel the plaster becoming stiff around his wrist, but tried to ignore the sensation.

"Alright, Mr. Wilkins." Came the voice of the nurse as she made her way back into the cubicle. "You can get going, now. Please stop by the desk to make an appointment to get the cast taken off, in about six to eight weeks."

"Thanks." Matthew smiled slightly at the nurse, and started to pull his shirt back on. The doctor had made him remove it while the x-rays were taken, but now he had to face the task of putting it back on and buttoning it, with fingers he now realised he could barely even wiggle. He managed to get it on over the cast, and pulled up over his shoulders, but he could manage no more. He was surprised at how much it still hurt, even with the cast wrapped around it. The doctor had also prescribed him some painkillers, but the one he had been given had not yet kicked in. "This is ridiculous, how is a guy supposed to do anything with this thing?"

"Here." Annie offered, and started to button the front of his shirt for him. He was impressed when she left the top two buttons undone, just as he normally wore his shirts.

"Thanks, Annie. I can't believe how useless I am. Sorry." He apologised, not really sure why he was doing so, but feeling he should anyway. "I can't even move my fingers, now. Is this supposed to be this tight?"

"Yes, it is." She replied, and he realised that she

must know by experience.

They left the emergency room together, stopping long enough for him to make an appointment to get the cast removed. He then led her to his car, and asked very nicely if she might consider driving him back to his apartment. He was greatly relieved when she said yes. He handed her the keys, and went to the passenger side door.

Sitting in the passenger seat reminded him of riding in the car with his grandfather. In those days, he couldn't even see over the dashboard, it was his earliest memory in fact. The sun had been bright, the roof was down, and the chrome gleamed so brightly it threatened to blind anyone who looked at it. That was a few weeks before they moved to the town where he had grown up, leaving his grandfather so far away. When he had finally received the keys to the car, he had put off driving it until another day when the sun was bright. For a while, he had thought that the car might bring the girls that his mother was so insistent he date, but it didn't. They still weren't interested in him. So he had decided he would wait until the right girl came his way. That turned out to be Annie.

"This is a great car." Annie commented.

"It was my grandfather's." He told her without elaboration. Annie drove toward his apartment block without even asking the way, as if she had memorised the route. She pulled into the parking lot under the building, parking the large car with ease.

"Do you need a hand?" She asked.

"No, I'll be fine thanks." He replied, immediately cursing himself for his own stupidity. They climbed out of the car, and she passed him back the keys. "Thanks, Annie, again. It's been a rather eventful day, and I'm rather looking forward to getting back to that marking, now. That's a lie; I'm just trying to convince myself. Do me a favour, Annie; watch out for Harley. I know now why I don't trust him."

"I don't intend to go any where near him. I think I'll just crawl into bed with a book, and try not to dream." She assured him. "And by the way, thanks for standing up for me. See you soon."

"Bye." He watched as she walked away from the car. He had the greatest urge to call out for her to come back, but he knew he couldn't. Instead, he made his way up to his apartment, where he made an attempt to mark all the papers he had spent all day so successfully avoiding, and which now demanded his full attention.

Chapter Twenty-four

I was shaken by the image before my eyes. Brace's silent form spread across the ground, injured but not dead. I crossed to him as Haltar disappeared into the trees that surrounded us. He was not aware that I had observed him, and his part in what had occurred. Silently, I placed my hands on Brace, trying to wake his body and to bring his soul back. Finally, his eyes opened.

"Anicia? What happened?" He asked me.

"Haltar hit you, I saw him do so." I told him

"My head, it hurts as if it were crushed." Brace cried.

"Come, we shall seek out Malarchy, he will know how to assist you, how to take the pain away." I assured him. I assisted him to his feet, and together we went in to the direction in which I had last seen Malarchy. We trod slowly and carefully towards the small clearing where Malarchy sat, singing our song softly as he sorted through the many ingredients his father needed. "Malarchy, quickly. Brace has been injured."

"How?" Malarchy asked.

"I believe that Haltar injured him. I replied quietly.

"Does it hurt?" Malarchy requested.

"Very much so, Malarchy. As if my head has been crushed. Haltar shows no care, no mercy, towards anyone. He sleeps with Alexis, yet still he wants to be joined to Anicia. We all can tell that the match is wrong, yet still he persists in pursuing not only Anicia, but also Alexis, to break my happiness as well as yours without regret. Please my friends, do not let this become your fates." Brace told us quietly.

"Well, for the pain in your head, I can help you, but for the pain in your heart, that will be harder, and it will be for you to do." Malarchy told him. I watched as Malarchy mixed several things together, pounding red berries with several different leaves, and the sweet nectar of a blossom. Finally, it was finished. Malarchy held it out for Brace, and he swallowed the thick pulp.

"It tastes foul, but I think I feel its effects already." Brace told him.

I sat between my two friends. Malarchy went back to his sweet humming, and I filled the air with the sweet words of our song. Brace seemed to listen contentedly, forgetting momentarily of his own worries, like the throbbing pain within his skull, and the pain of heartache within his chest.

Chapter Twenty-five

He had been seriously thinking about asking her to marry him. He had been dating Carlene for a long time now. Annie had pushed them closer and closer together, and finally, they had fallen in love. He was absolutely sure that they would be together forever.

André had been sitting, thinking about it for hours now. When Gary had come in for a few minutes before heading out again, he had asked his friend what he thought of the idea. He had thought it was a great plan right away, but André had sworn him to secrecy, knowing that although Annie would be happy for him, he did not want her to know until he was ready. Apparently, Gary shared Annie's view that they were meant to be together.

Of course, he realised, this meant he would have

to take her home again. He wasn't so sure of his mother's reaction to her after their first meeting. But it could not be avoided, because he would have to get the rings. They had been his father's mother's, old diamonds on a band of white gold, which would be perfect on Carlene's slender finger. The yellow diamond that would one day be his sister's was far more valuable, but the stone was too large for Carlene. Mind you, he wasn't sure Annie's ring would fit her, because there was very little structure to Annie's left hand after it got crushed.

Now his only worry was when and how to ask her. He toyed with the idea of some cheesy proposal in a fancy restaurant, but he wasn't sure that was his style. He might just slip it in to conversation sometime, casually as if it had only just occurred to him. His best idea so far was to kick Gary out for the night, get her over to the frat house, and woo her with chocolates, flowers and romance. It may not be much better than the cheesy restaurant idea, but he was willing to keep it his favourite option so far. Then he set about rehearsing what he would say to her. This actually seemed to be a harder task than figuring out *where* he would ask her.

"Carlene, I love you, and I always will. Marry me, my heart." He tried. "Well that sucks.

"Carlene, we are in love. I have always believed that when two people are in love, they should show it. Therefore, I would be greatly honoured if you would be my bride. Okay, I sound like some nineteenth century idiot now.

"Carlene, marry me." He smiled to himself. "That's the one."

He knew he wanted her to say yes more than he had ever wanted anything in his life. She had to say yes, she just had to. She would say yes, after all, it was where they had been heading for a long time. They both knew it.

Out in the hall, the phone was ringing. André refused to get a cell phone, and instead depended on the house phone for all messages. Therefore, he was not surprised when one of the guys called to him that there was someone wanting to talk. He made his way to the phone as swiftly as he could be bothered to, already sensing that it was Carlene.

"Hello?" He called into the receiver, waiting for her sweet voice to reply.

"Hey, baby, it's me. I've got a little problem about tonight. Harley was in a fight, he just got home, and he won't tell me who it was with. All he says is the other guy deserved it, but that isn't much for me to go on. I'm sorry, honey, but I really don't think I can leave him tonight. He's being a bit of a baby, tells me he wants his big sister to take care of him. I know it's pathetic, but I do like to keep him happy as best I can." Carlene explained. He felt a little disappointed, but knew that she would not blow him off normally. And she *did* sound disappointed herself. He could have killed Harley, but instead he pictured her, and forgave her instantly.

"No worries, sweetheart, we'll get together next weekend anyway, right?" He smiled, knowing he was going to be ready by then.

"Sure thing. Love you, baby. Bye."

"Bye, honey." He hung up the phone and went back into his room. He was at a loose end now, but all he could bring himself to do was to turn on his TV, and watch reruns of Gilligan's Island.

Chapter Twenty-six

The anger was surging around his body, his veins full of pulsating, angry blood. He had never been so frustrated in his whole life. How dare that bitch do that to him again? She would never get another chance, that was for sure. He would not give her the satisfaction of getting away with it this time, either. They would both have to pay, a great deal more this time than the last.

As Carlene had dabbed at his face with peroxide and iodine, he had tried to ignore the fire that they brought to his skin. Harley knew right away that there would be marks left by the bitch's fingernails. He thought back, and smiled with some satisfaction over the fact that he had managed to break the wrist of the jerk that was trying to defend her. But that was not before he had been hit. There was now a large purple and black bruise forming over his right eye. He winced as he touched it, checking the tenderness of the skin.

Carlene had, of course, questioned him about how he had been injured, wanting to know who he had been fighting with. She was persistent, but he had refused to say anything, knowing that he would receive her damnation for fighting with the sister of the guy she was dating. Of course, if he had his own way, he would put a stop to their little relationship straight away. He didn't like that stuck up prick any more than he liked the jerk that Annie seemed to be seeing every time *he* was supposed to be on a date with her. Unfortunately, they seemed to be in love. Worse than that, it was one of those nauseating loves that meant they walked barefoot in the park, held hands, kissed in public. The thought of it was enough to make him feel ill. Of course, everyone else thought they made the perfect couple, but no one would be able to convince him of the fact.

"Hey Harley, did you hear what happened to André's friend Barry?" Carlene called through the door to him.

"Yeah, it's terrible. You think you'll be safe in a swimming pool, but I guess you're not safe anywhere these days." He called back. His immediate thought was to worry in case he had been seen, but there was no way he could have been, was there?

"They're looking for the guy who did it. They reckon he must be fairly athletic looking, cause no one noticed him coming or going. They've got cameras, but apparently the tapes are all fuzzy." Carlene told him. He let out the breath that he suddenly realised he had been holding. He knew there wouldn't be any real problem in that department. He realised once more that he could normally get away with murder if he felt like it.

"Hey, Carlene, why don't we order pizza, I've got a craving for pepperoni, and I'm suddenly starving." He told her as he came out of the bathroom and sat on the couch. He let out a small yelp as he leaned back against the seat.

"Does it hurt?" Carlene asked, looking concerned, just as he hoped she would.

"It's not so bad, really." He replied, trying hard to wince as he spoke. He rather liked the sympathy he was getting from her. As she called for the pizza, Harley turned on the TV, and revelled in all the attention he was receiving.

Chapter Twenty-seven

At 7pm on Monday, Annie walked into the coffee house with Gary at her side. Their presence there had been requested by Jalena Carmichael, and Annie had been sworn to secrecy. Jalena wanted Gary to meet her parents before the inevitable first date even happened. Luckily, it was Monday, because it seemed to be the only evening when the coffee house was really quiet. All the other students had spent so long partying over the weekend, that they normally put off their studies until the last minute, and for some reason, most of the time, assignments were due on Tuesdays.

Annie recognised Jalena's parents instantly, and made her way to where they were sitting, greeting them as if she had already known them for years. Jalena was, as usual, rushing about, even though there were only a couple of girls in one corner, and a group of fluffy chin guys, six or seven of them, by the window, discussing the merits of Milton's 'Paradise Regained'. In their opinions, it was over rated.

"Hi, you must be Mr. and Mrs. Carmichael." Annie greeted, already knowing the answer. "I'm Annie Bouvais, and this is my good friend Gary Hutchins."

"Nice to meet you." Gary smiled. They chatted for several minutes about the coffee house, and Jalena, before she joined them.

"Sorry, I know it doesn't look busy, but it just never seems to stop. I think the owner must have realised that this place was a gold mine before he sent me here. You wouldn't believe the profits in coffee! Here, there's hot chocolate for Annie, coffee for Gary - it's a new Costa Rican blend I'm trialing, it's pretty good, and I managed to get a good deal on the beans. Mom, English breakfast as always, and decaf for Dad." Jalena greeted, handing cups around the group. Annie noticed that her drink was already dusted with cinnamon, just how she liked it.

"We were just talking about college, Jalena." Her mother said pointedly. "Apparently, you can just listen in on lessons if you like."

"Classes, mom, and I don't have the time." Jalena sighed.

"But it wouldn't cost you anything, sweetheart." Her mother continued. "Not a penny."

"I still don't have the time, mom. I have a full time job here, you know, and Mr. Mewes employed me to manage this place. I can't leave it all for that spotty kid to handle. Maybe I'll go back to college one day, but until I can afford to study without having a full time job, it will just have to wait. I can't see any point in just listening to classes I can't even benefit from." Jalena told her mother firmly.

"But sweetheart, someone with SAT scores as high as yours should be doing something better with their lives. You *should* be in college." Mrs. Carmichael pushed, then turned to Annie and Gary. "You know, she got a combined 1500"

"That's fantastic!" Annie smiled. *Stick that in your pipe and smoke it, André!* She thought. She had always got the feeling that Jalena should be doing something far more intellectual with her self, but yet again, her soul was a victim of circumstances. She glanced at Gary, and found a new look of awe on his face. He noticed her glance, and returned it with a smile. She rolled her eyes, and as they made their way back to the group, she noticed Matthew Wilkins entering the coffee house. She was sure she could feel her face turn red as she diverted her gaze.

"You'll have to stop that if you don't want him to guess." Gary whispered in her ear, a gentle mock in his tone.

"Are you trying to get me in trouble?" She hissed back at him, giving him a gentle nudge, and a conspiratorial wink. It never ceased to amaze her just how much her friend knew without even asking, how much he could understand without the slightest hint from her.

"Hey Mr. Wilkins, how's the wrist?" One of the girls from the corner called to him as he headed across the room.

"Still broken." He called back jovially, holding up his arm as some sort of proof. He continued over to where they were sitting, a smile still on his face. "Hi, sorry to pull you away Jalena, could I get a coffee?"

"Sure thing. Sit yourself down, right there next to Gary, and I'll get it for you. I have a good deal on Costa Rica finest today, if I can interest you in that. It's good, and cheap, too." Jalena smiled back.

"Sounds great." He agreed, and took the seat next to Gary as she had suggested.

"So, how's the wrist really?" Annie asked, feeling self conscious about the concern that her voice held.

"Not too bad, except itchy, and the drugs the doctor gave me make me a little light headed once they kick in – I think they may have made me a little giggly when I had my meeting with Hathaway this afternoon, but I doubt she noticed it. The best thing is that I no longer have to mark the Mitchell papers. He told me there was no way I could write legibly, so he let me off. I didn't have the heart to tell him I can write left handed, too." He admitted. "It meant that I was at a loose end this evening, so here I am."

"And look, everyone seems to have signed your wrist, how sweet." Mrs. Carmichael observed.

"Sorry, Mr. and Mrs. Carmichael, this is Mr. Wilkins, he's a teacher here, of anthropology." Annie introduced.

"That sounds interesting. Wasn't Jalena interested in anthropology at one time?" Mrs. Carmichael asked her husband.

"No dear, it was astrology, but I'm sure a lot of people make the same mistake." He corrected her gently.

"Still, I'm sure she must be interested. Our Jalena is a bright one. So very bright." Mrs. Carmichael continued wistfully, watching her daughter. Annie got the feeling that Jalena's mother was more disappointed by her daughter's situation than Jalena was. "Don't you think, Mr. Wilkins, that it is a shame to let intellect go to waste?"

"Yes, I do, and please, call me Matthew. I've already offered Jalena access to my classes, but she always tells me she doesn't have the time. She's near enough to being a genius, and I'd be happy to have her there, but she insists she is too busy." Matthew responded. Annie could detect in his voice that he, too, felt that Jalena was wasted as a waitress.

"Mom, please, stop." Jalena requested gently, as she returned with a large cup of coffee, which she offered to Matthew. He moved to take it with his right hand, before he realised that he could not. He laughed, and took it with his left hand instead. "Could we please talk about something else, now, because as I have told all of you already, I really *don't* have the time for college with a full time job, and I can't afford it without one."

The conversation was now most definitely closed, and so it moved on to other subjects. A while later, Jalena bought out a birthday cake for her father, and they all sang. The cake was offered around the coffee house to all the customers, which now included a group of kids who had obviously been out at the black hole, because they smelt strongly of smoke and alcohol. Eventually, Jalena's parents excused themselves, and Jalena went back to working, trying to clean away the debris of the day.

"How is Barry?" Matthew asked just after Jalena stepped away.

"Not so bad. They sent him home this afternoon." Gary responded, not really paying attention to anything, as he watched Jalena working. "Excuse me, I'll be right back."

"Has he asked her out yet?" Matthew asked as they watched Gary go after Jalena.

"No, he's being stubborn." Annie replied absentmindedly, then turned to look at him, a little surprised.

"It's kind of obvious." He grinned, reading her expression with ease. She couldn't help but smile at him.

"I know it is to me, but I didn't think it was to anyone else." She admitted, wondering if this meant that Matthew Wilkins might know more than he was letting on. "What did Professor Mitchell say when you told him you only managed to grade three of those papers?"

"He wasn't impressed. I managed to get another dozen or so done last night, but the stack was still this high." He replied, then started to run his fingernails along the edge of the cast closest to his fingers. "Is it supposed to itch this much?"

"You don't get to complain until the cast has been on for at least three weeks. Trust me, when you have spent a couple of months with your hand wrapped in all sorts of bandaging, you'll understand." She told him knowingly, recalling the months she had spent with her hand wrapped in plaster, followed by months of physiotherapy that never fulfilled its promise. "Try plastic rulers, they're great for the nubbly bones just above the wrist."

"Thanks, I'll bear that in mind." Matthew smiled. It was getting late, and many of the other customers had already departed. The fluffy chin guys had given up their argument about literature, and left. The girls who were giggling in the corner had cleared out, too. The black hole crew was still hanging on, but was starting to flag a little. Gary was now helping Jalena to tidy up, so Annie was near enough alone with Matthew.

"Is there anything specific that I'm going to need next weekend?" She asked him.

"Not really. It'll be warm, so light clothes, and a sweater for night. It can get a little chilly once it gets dark. I would have suggested a good book for the ride, but there is no way I can drive. This thing holds my fingers so straight, I can't even wiggle them. There's no way that I can change gears." He answered, again itching his hand distractedly.

"It's a good thing I can drive a stick shift." Annie commented. "Are you sure I don't have to pay anything?"

"I'm sure. The doc loves to help girls in distress, and I can't remember the last time he actually asked for money for that particular use of his talents. You won't need much money, anyway. There's not much to buy. Just bring yourself, and we'll get these dreams of yours explained once and for all." He assured her. She looked up just in time to notice Gary on his way back to the table. Jalena had obviously gotten exasperated with him, and had sent him away, but he was still grinning widely.

"It's getting late." Annie sighed, looking at her watch. "I should really get going."

"Not on your own, you won't." Gary responded quickly. Annie started to protest, but Matthew cut her short.

"He's right, Annie. There's someone out there hurting people." Matthew agreed, and stroked his left hand across his cast. She knew exactly what he was getting at, but it was only just occurring to her. If anyone was at risk, she was.

"Okay, then, what do you two suggest?" She

challenged, looking from one to the other and back again.

"Gary will stay here, with Jalena, until she closes, and he'll take her up to her apartment, too. I'll walk you home." Matthew told her firmly.

"That's great, genius, but who'll protect you when you walk home, or Gary when he walks home?" Annie laughed derisively.

"We're guys, we can look after ourselves." Gary pointed out, but Annie was not convinced by this as an argument.

"We'll take our chances, Annie." Matthew assured her, standing up and waiting for her to make some sort of move. "Come on. I'm not going to let anyone take any chances unless they have to."

"Okay, okay. Gary, I'll see you later, sweetie." Annie agreed finally, giving her friend a quick hug, then made her way to the door, Matthew following behind her.

For some reason, tonight she was nervous walking alone with Matthew. Maybe it was because she knew there was a chance that Harley was out there somewhere, waiting for them in the shadows. She knew that part of his problem had to be that they had embarrassed him that first evening in the coffee house, that they had probably compounded that by fighting with him at the hospital, but there wasn't anything they could do to take it back, now. She was also nervous about walking alone with him so late, even though it wasn't the first time they had walked alone together. Some how, she found herself babbling about nothing at all, except the weather, which she found herself talking about most of the way there. She could hardly believe how stupid she sounded, even to herself.

"Would you like to come in for a coffee? My

roommate is away at the moment, and the place is kind of creepy this time of night." She asked as they got to her door.

"Sure, but I can't stay long. I'm in class at 8:30 in the morning." Matthew accepted. She unlocked the door, and they stepped into the living room area. There was moonlight coming through the window, so it was a moment before Annie switched on the light.

"Make yourself comfortable." Annie told Matthew as she flicked the switch. She heard the sharp intake of his breath before he really even took it. "What is it?"

"Take a look." He breathed. She turned around, and felt the breath catch in her own throat.

Chapter Twenty-eight

He had never seen anything quite like it before. Annie's photograph was pinned to the door with a heavy cleaver, her face scratched from its surface. The word 'bitch' had been carved into the door.

"How did he get in?" Annie whispered.

"Could he have got a key from somewhere?" He asked shakily, feeling a little sickened.

"I don't think so. André has a key, I guess Harley could've got it, without him realising it was gone. It has to have been Harley, doesn't it?" Annie cried.

"Who else could it have been, for Christ's sake? I don't like this Annie, at all. There is no way I can leave you here if he can get in. He managed it once, he'll do it again." He told her sternly. He looked at her unsmiling face, a questioning look in her eyes. "There has to be someplace you can go, Annie."

"Well, André shares a room, with Gary. Jalena has her parents staying the night. Carlene would demand an explanation from me, which I obviously can't offer her because it happens to be *her* brother who has turned homicidal maniac. Those are all the people that I know, I'm afraid. So, unless you can think of anything better, then I have no other options but to stay here." Annie replied. He did have an idea, but he was afraid to even voice it. Then again, what choice did he have?

"You know me. I know what you're thinking, and I appreciate the fact that this goes against almost every single one of the rules that you are so scared of, but there is no way that I am leaving this room without you. It's just for one night, then you can go stay with someone else, anyone else. But tonight, I'm not giving you another option." He told her firmly. Her face told him her doubts, but he stood firm.

"I really don't think that's a good idea." She looked at him doubtfully.

"I don't care. He's insane, Annie, and there is nothing that either of us can do to prove it, so as I said, I am not leaving you here. Get your things, whatever you'll need for tonight and tomorrow." He told her.

"Alright." She agreed finally. He waited as she collected several things from her room, returning with a small hold all and a book bag. She quickly scrawled a note to her roommate across a piece of paper:

> *'Joanna, gone away for a few days.*
> *See you soon, Annie'*

Matthew watched her as she pinned the note to the cork

notice board on the wall in the small kitchen area. Then they left.

They made their way out of the building as quickly as possible. There was no way he could take the chance that they would be seen in this situation, if not for his own sake, then for Annie's. It was late, and there was no way that they could explain the situation if they *were* spotted. Still, he led her to his apartment, across the fields, over the bridge, and to the building where he lived.

As he unlocked the door, he held his breath. There was no way that Harley could've got into his apartment, but he still braced himself in case there was a message carved into *his* wall. He realised that Annie was doing the same, but as he flicked on the light, he knew it was safe, that there was nothing there. A light breeze greeted them, flowing through the open window in his bedroom. He crossed to it quickly, and pulled it shut, before moving the telescope away to the other side of the room.

"You take the bed, I'll sleep on the couch." He decided, realising that he was probably going to need to be pulled out of the thing in the morning after he sank into its depths. Annie nodded, and moved into the bedroom. There was no door in the frame, only his dream catcher, given to him by a young girl of eight who he had taught to read and write. She had been labelled as un-teachable by the local grade school, but he had spent hours with her, one to one, and by the end of a year, she had been able to read anything, and write whatever she chose. She had constructed the dream catcher herself, threading the nuggets of turquoise onto the web of the structure, and binding the three eagle feathers to the bottom of the ring along with a small piece of fur. It was one of the few things in the apartment that actually belonged to him.

"Thanks, Matthew. You were right, I couldn't have stayed there on my own, tonight." Annie smiled at him gently. He pulled an old blanket from the closet, and a pair of jogging pants from a drawer at the bottom of the bureau. Then he made his way back out to the couch, regretting the fact that he hadn't bought his own instead of using the one that came with the apartment. He went to the small bathroom, and changed into the jogging pants. He washed his face, cleaned his teeth, and then went back to the couch.

"Help yourself to anything you need Annie, make yourself at home." He called to her. She appeared a few moments later, dressed in dark blue satin pyjamas, her thick, dark hair plaited down her back and tied with a ribbon that matched. He looked at her for the briefest of moments, surprised once more by her beauty, before he averted his eyes. She was carrying a face cloth, and a toothbrush, and moved silently to the bathroom. He could hear her brushing her teeth. When she came back out, she had a dreamy smile on her face, her eyes a little out of focus, and made her way back to the bedroom.

"Good night, Matthew, and thanks again." She said as she moved through the doorway. He watched as she pulled back the bed sheets, and climbed into the bed.

"Good night Annie, and don't dream." He called to her, feeling himself sinking a little. He shifted slightly, and closed his eyes. He was asleep within a few minutes, finally knowing what it was like to say goodnight to Annie for real.

Chapter Twenty-nine

The following day, Annie went to stay with Jalena, telling her that she had a problem in her dorm room. She had to go back to pick up some more bits and pieces, but she didn't hang around for long. She had felt so apprehensive going back in there, terrified that she might find Harley waiting for her, then clobbering her, or attacking her with the cleaver. She didn't like those possibilities. There was no way she could take the chance that he would be there, so she took as much as she thought she would need until Friday.

She spent the week keeping as out of sight as she possibly could. She attended her lectures, except for Matthew's. He had told her not to worry, that she had enough to cope with, that she needn't have to worry about learning a load of lies until after they had had a chance to get to the bottom of things.

When she was not in lectures, she stayed in Jalena's apartment, or in the coffee house. She even helped out a little when it got busy. She was having fun, until Thursday, when Jalena apologised to her that she couldn't stay another night. Her pipe had burst, and she had to vacate for the night as well.

"You can come back tomorrow." Jalena promised. Annie told Jalena not to worry, that she would be able to go someplace else.

When she arrived back at Matthew's apartment, he let her back in without too much persuasion. She knew the situation was bad, but she couldn't think what else to do. When he went out for a while, leaving her alone in the apartment, she spent a long time just looking out of the window in the bedroom. She had watched him make his way to the dorm house, his route looking so different from this new viewpoint. The telescope that she had noticed before was now next to the window, and by pointing it in the right direction, and focusing the lens, she could look directly into her own bedroom

The following morning, both Annie and Matthew returned to the dorm room. The cleaver was still there, embedded into the door. The word scratched into the wood was even more visible in the bright morning sunlight than it had been before.

They were going to be leaving late that afternoon for the journey down to Matthew's hometown. He had been to the stores on his way back from is meeting the evening before, and had bought food and drinks for the drive down and back. Annie may have agreed to do the driving, but she was now growing a little apprehensive about the journey, and where they were to end up.

Annie packed a couple sweaters, a pair of jeans, and her favourite summer dress. She also packed a couple of shirts, underwear, and socks. Light make-ups and perfumes littered the desk that doubled as dressing table. She selected several items, and put them into her old red suitcase with her clothes. She hummed as she did so, some song she knew from somewhere, but couldn't remember where.

When she was done, she went out to the living room area, where she found Matthew sitting, looking at the cleaver in the door. She smiled slightly at his intense gazing as she moved into the kitchen and put the teakettle on. She made two cups of tea, and carried them over.

"What time did you say you had a lecture?" She asked him.

"My first is at 11:30, then there's another one at 2. I'll be done there by 5, then I've got my meeting with Hathaway. You'd think she'd be bored of my progress by now, but apparently not. It never takes long, so we can be on the road by 7 or so. All being well, by this time tomorrow, we can get rid of the fear that accompanies your dreams." He replied. She looked at him, a little surprised that he understood the fear she felt.

"I hope so." She said simply.

A short while later, they were ready to go. Annie finally pulled the large, heavy cleaver from the door, and crumpled the damaged photograph in her hand. She pulled the first note she had left from the board in the kitchen, and quickly scribbled another:

Joanna, gone on trip with
Anthro. class. See you Sunday
Annie

They left together, and only parted once they got outside. Annie watched as Matthew walked away toward the lecture halls where he would spend much of the day. She, on the other hand, turned toward his apartment, and started walking. Her small red case was surprisingly heavy, and she hoped that she had packed the right things for a weekend where she would hopefully find some answers. She was struggling with the case, and had made it about halfway when she met Jalena.

"Please tell me you found somewhere to sleep last night!" Jalena exclaimed when they met.

"Yeah, no problem. And while we're on the subject, I'm fine for tonight, too. I'm going on a class trip for anthropology for the weekend, and we're off this evening." Annie explained.

"With the lovely Matthew, by any chance?" Jalena smiled slyly.

"Uh, yeah. Actually, I'm on my way to his apartment now to drop my case off, then I was going to drop in for my hot chocolate." She lied. Her intention had been to stay in Matthew's apartment all day.

"You have his keys? How did you manage that? If I had the keys to Gary's place, I'd be there in a shot, hoping I got caught by him, like in one of those cruddy romance novels my friend used to read. I can picture it now, all sweaty and hot like a night in the middle of summer. Okay, my imagination sometimes runs away. Can I come with you?" Jalena asked. "I love seeing where other people come from, and where they go when they're done with their days."

"I don't know, I think he trusts me, for some reason. And I don't think he imagines coming back to find me in any kind of romance novel situation." Annie looked at her doubtfully.

"Of course he doesn't, and you'll be with me, so it's all good. Come on, what harm can come of it?" Jalena giggled. "Besides, you said yourself that you were coming to the coffee house after you'd been there, so I might as well come with you, and we can go together. I'll even help carry your bag if you like."

"Sure, I guess you're right. Don't worry, my case isn't that bad, it's just I can only carry it in my right hand, 'cause I can't take weight in my left hand." Annie finally agreed. She picked her case back up, and remembered just how heavy it was.

"Why can't you carry weight in your left hand?" Jalena asked.

"I had an accident when I was a kid. My hand got crushed when a rather large car drove over it, after it hit me and knocked me to the ground. They managed to fix the bones, but the muscles never really regained the ground they had lost. If you look real close, you can see the difference in them." Annie explained as they walked. They were at the bridge, and Annie could see the apartment building now.

"I hope they locked the driver up." Jalena sounded a little shocked by this new revelation.

"No, actually, they never got caught. Daddy was dead by then, and mom didn't have the strength to fight for them to keep looking. In the end, it didn't really make any difference, anyway. You know that old joke about never being able to play the violin again? Well, it was a little bit of a reality. I can still manage for a little while, but not for the hours I used to. They tell me I had potential, still do have talent, apparently, but it makes no difference, because I just can't do it anymore." Annie continued with her tale.

"I'm sorry."

"Don't be sorry, Jalena. I came to terms with it a long time ago. I don't even think about it much any more." Annie admitted. They were now climbing the stairway up to Matthew's apartment. At the top, Annie led Jalena along the corridor, to the door. She had the keys to the car and the apartment in her pocket, and now used them to unlock the door. She placed her case just inside the door, and then moved to the desk to leave a note, making some attempt at pretending she had never been there before. She rummaged for a pen and paper, then scribbled a note, keeping Jalena waiting just long enough. She knew that she would be back before he would. "Come on, lets get out of here."

Chapter Thirty

There was a cool breeze coming in through the car's open window. They had been on the road for nearly three hours now, although they had stopped, to refuel the car, for nearly twenty minutes. Annie enjoyed driving the car, and had felt at home behind the wheel from the moment the houses either side of the highway had started to thin out. She was no longer worried about being spotted behind the wheel, that some one might see them, and that danger would be waiting for them around the next bend in the rather oddly straight road.

When they had stopped at the Gasoramma, she had tried to keep her mind from wandering to the place that imagined that Matthew Wilkins was taking her to meet his parents rather than where she was being taken for experimentation, which is what she had started to think might be the case. In fact, Matthew's encouraging smile was the only thing that kept her from turning the car around and making their way back home.

Now that they were back on the open road, all thoughts of that were driven from her mind. They were a fair way into New Mexico when Matthew started to hum a tune that Annie found remarkably familiar. It was the same tune that she had been humming earlier that day, the tune that had been running around her head, filling her spare waking minutes for the last few weeks. It took her a few moments to realise that she was singing the words that went with the tune.

The words were soft and sweet, naïve at times, but always right. They filled the car with their melodious notes. As the words ended, they both fell silent. Annie was trying to find an explanation for what had just happened, because as far as she was concerned, the song was only known to her. They had driven in silence for almost ten minutes before Matthew finally spoke again.

"How did you know those words?" He asked, looking at her. She could feel his blue eyes looking at her, boring into her, and glanced at him just long enough to confirm that they were.

"I don't know, they were just there. I must have heard them somewhere before, on the radio or something." She replied, knowing that her answer was a lie.

"Possible, but not very convincing. It's okay; I don't need you to tell me. Maybe I heard you humming it at some point. Maybe you hum in your sleep!" He grinned. She nodded, but at some level, she knew the answer to his question. He knew the song the same way that she did. "If you find a name for it, I'll Google it when we get back."

"I don't think there is a name for it." She told him with certainty. After all, did songs have names that long ago? "But I'll let you know."

The rest of the journey was quiet. Matthew spent a while trying to wiggle his fingers, without much success, because the cast was holding them too straight. All he could manage was to move the very tips of them backwards and forwards. At one point, she noticed he was trying so hard that he was making his ears wiggle instead. She suppressed a giggle, and it turned into a yawn that was only half pretend.

"Not much further now." He told her.

The closer they got, the more apprehensive Annie felt. She had been able to tell him everything for a reason. She had trusted him since the first time he had spoken to her, or perhaps even for longer than that. Maybe she had even trusted him from the very first moment she had seen him, because she had known him in that instant, without any doubt.

"Are you scared?" He asked, and she wondered if he might be reading her thoughts.

"What of?" She asked back.

"Finding the truth, a past that you don't like. I would be terrified if it were me, I think. I like not knowing anything, most of the time, at any rate." He replied thoughtfully. "But I get why you need to know. Maybe if they were my dreams, then I'd want to know, too."

"I think you'd already know. I think you know all the answers to my secrets already, you're just not telling me what they are." She was trying to sound light, but her words were more truthful than she was willing to let on. "Actually, I'm a little scared of meeting your parents."

"Hah!" He laughed loudly. "You have every right to be. My mother eats small children for breakfast, and my father is a complete scoundrel."

"Stop it!" Annie protested, laughing herself.

"No, of course, you're right again." He admitted. "Dad is a doctor, but the dull kind, who calls me 'son' - which I've always hated. Mom is a proper housewife, who spends all her time making sure her hair is perfect, her clothes match, and everyone is fed to bursting. Believe me, you will never go hungry in the Wilkins' house. When fall comes, my dad will take a hunting trip, and mom will spend the winter feeding him the stuff he manages to kill. It's almost enough to turn you vegetarian, until mom starts cooking bacon on a Saturday morning, because she cooks *amazing* bacon."

"Your family means a lot to you." Annie smiled, knowing that her friends were just as important to her.

"Does that make me soft?" He asked, a note of worry in his voice.

"No, it makes you human." She assured him. They fell silent again, driving onwards through the dark.

At almost one am, they reached the outskirts of a town. A sign at a crossroads indicated the way up to the reservation, where Annie assumed she would be driving them the following morning. All along the highway there were dark buildings sitting silently in the night, a few with porch lights illuminated in case a late caller might appear. A motel was lit up with neon, flashing the word vacancy in blue letters, but any would be visitors were out of luck, because the desk clerk's office was dark.

Matthew started to direct her through the dark streets with the ease of someone who had grown up on them. When he told her to take a narrow road, she did so, even though it seemed barely wide enough for the car to slide through.

"It gets wider at the end." He assured her. And sure enough, the road opened out enough for her to turn the car. A single light shone at the end of the street, and beyond the pulled shades, there was the flicker of a television set. "That's the one."

Annie swung the car around, and pulled up outside the house. She cut the ignition, and silence greeted them. A minute passed before they both started to laugh nervously.

"I'll go first." Matthew said finally. "I told mom we were coming, but she's probably forgotten by now."

He climbed out of the car, and she watched him as he raced up the walkway to the house. He rang the bell, and waited, running his un-plastered hand over the wooden pole that was supporting the porch. She could tell he was pleased to be home, even if it would be for only a few days. A minute passed before a woman opened the door. Her hair was like liquid caramel, falling around her shoulders, and she was dressed in a blue pantsuit that radiated her social standing. Matthew bent a little, and kissed his mother on the cheek, then turned and raised his plastered hand in a wave. Annie smiled and waved back. As he bounded back to the car, she couldn't help but wonder what he was so excited about.

"Come on, you can't sleep in the car!" He told her as he pulled open the car door for her. Actually, she thought she could have slept very comfortably in the car's bench seats, but she wasn't about to argue, as Matthew was already retrieving her red case from the trunk. He led her up the walkway to the house, a huge smile across his face. "Mom, I'd like you to meet Annie Bouvais.

Annie, this is my mom."

"Well, aren't you just the prettiest thing! Come on in. Ben is in the den, watching the Late, Late show, just to prove how late it is, Matthew." His mother smiled sincerely. Matthew looked a little sheepish, but he followed his mother, still carrying Annie's case. "Ben, Matthew is here, and he's bought a friend with him."

"Good to see you, son." Ben Wilkins greeted, standing from his easy chair, and extending his hand toward his son. Matthew turned to Annie, and rolled his eyes, but took his hand anyway. "And who might this be?"

"Annie Bouvais." Annie offered, as her hand was taken and clasped warmly. "Nice to meet you, both."

"Well, any friend of Matthew's is always welcome here." Mrs. Wilkins told her, a flash of her perfect white teeth almost blinding her.

"I must admit, I'm absolutely bushed, and I didn't even drive. We're due to see the doc fairly early in the morning, so I guess we'd better turn in. Annie, I'll show you the spare room." Matthew yawned.

"I'll take a look at that wrist for you tomorrow, too, son." Ben Wilkins told his son as Matthew led Annie up the stairs to the spare bedroom.

"Didn't I warn you?" He whispered conspiratorially. "I Know I'm his son, does he *have* to keep reminding me? Any way, this is you, and that is me. I'm right across the hall if you need me for anything, and I must be a light sleeper, because you hum in your sleep, and I can hear you."

"I do not!" She giggled. "Thank you, Matthew."

"Good night, Annie."

"Good night."

Chapter Thirty-one

Her apartment was cold. She couldn't remember turning the thermostat down. She flicked on the light switch, and regretted it instantly.

The male form seated squarely on the over stuffed couch was one that she didn't know very well. She had only met him a couple of times, but that was enough. She knew that he was bad news the very first time she met him.

Her cat was sitting on the floor under the TV, hissing loudly at him. Jalena had never been quite so scared before.

"Where is she?" He growled in a low voice that was almost something from the most frightening nightmare she had ever had.

"Who?" She asked tentatively.

"Annie. Who else would I be looking for in this dive?" He demanded.

"I don't know." She cried, suddenly wishing she could be home in her bedroom, her parents downstairs, even if it did mean she would have to put up with her four younger brothers.

"You're a liar, Honey." He told her. Then his hands were wrapped around her throat, and it was all she could do to beg him to stop so she could tell him what little she knew.

Chapter Thirty-two

He knew exactly where to go, where he would find her. The girl had had very little resistance against his methods of persuasion, and she had still been breathing when he left her. Luckily, she hadn't been stupid enough to try and hold out on telling him what he wanted to know.

Now he knew where Annie was, he had to get to her. The ideal way would have been by car, but he didn't own one. Instead, he decided that stealing one would have to do. It was very easy to do, since not many of the cars had alarms, and most of them were not even locked. He finally picked out a green Honda. The door was easily pulled open, then he flicked down the sunshade. Some people were so stupid that they actually kept their keys tucked there. The driver of the Honda was one of those people. The key to the ignition fell straight in to his hand.

The car started immediately, and he drove straight out of the parking lot and onto the road. He took the interstate due south as the buildings became further apart. At midnight, he crossed the state line into New Mexico.

He had the name of the town written on the back of his hand where he could see it as he drove. He found himself smiling back from the rear view mirror, almost evilly. He had already decided what he was going to do to them. He would start by embarrassing them, just like they had done to him. He would make sure that her face never smiled again when she thought about that teacher of hers. He may make sure she would never smile *ever* again.

He stopped at an all night service station at around one am. He put a little gas in the car, then went into the store that served the pumps. There was a guy at the counter, some useless till jockey who had nothing better to do with his life than to work nights there. At that moment, he appeared to be reading one of the top shelf magazines, eating Nutter-butters from a pack on the counter. He guessed that the guy made regular trips to the rest rooms when he was working late because of those magazines.

"Hi, can I help you?" The clerk asked.

"Yeah, I'll take a carton of 'Lucky Strikes', and some matches. Put them on my tab." He told the clerk.

"We don't carry credit accounts." The boy told him uncertainly.

"Oh dear, and I'm all out of money. What do you suggest I do, then?" He smiled evilly once more.

"Well, you could go home without them." The young boy mumbled.

"Excuse me?" He boomed, impressed by his own

voice.

"I said you could leave without them." The boy said a little more loudly.

"Ah, well, you see, there are a couple of reasons why that won't work. The most important one is the gas I already put in my car." He smiled again, and watched the boy tremble. His magazine lay open on the counter, and he took notice of the skimpily clad women, mostly only clad below the waist if at all. One of the faces in particular leapt out at him from the page. Her long blond hair surrounded her face, falling around her bare shoulders. She was cupping her breasts, oversized as they were, her lips pouted and slightly apart. He knew the shape of her, and the feel of her skin next to his. Ali Rice.

"She's my favourite." The clerk said, pointing at Ali, obviously reading the expression on Harley's face.

"Mine too." He nodded.

The gun in his pocket suddenly felt heavier. It had come in handy the week before when he had been at the swimming pool. The cool, hard metal butt of the gun had made a perfect blunt object. He'd never shot a person before, but there was a first time for everything, and he was quite willing to do what he had to. Now there were three people who deserved the punishment of the gun's fury.

"D'you know what? You see, I know her. Oh the way she feels when she rides me, like nothing else you could imagine." He told the clerk, pulling the gun smoothly from his pocket. He toyed with the weapon, turning it over and over in his hand. He pulled the clip out, and checked the bullets. "Pretty thing, even if her titties are fake. I'm not sure she'll be pretty for too much longer, though." *Oh dear,* he thought, *now it'll have to be four.* "And now you know about it, too, so I'm really very sorry, but I'll have to make sure you can't talk about it. So, good bye."

The shot reverberated around the store. He smiled down at the body on the floor, and found himself laughing loudly. He didn't leave the store straight away, but instead made his way around, picking up a few bits that he decided might make his night a little better. There was a chiller cabinet at the back of the store, and he helped himself to a six-pack of beers. He grabbed some candy bars, and a few of the magazines, including the one from the counter. Finally, he made his way back out into the night, and climbed back into the car.

He drove on through the night, and finally arrived in the town at just after half past four in the morning. He found a dusty outcrop above the town in the hills, where he sat, drinking his beers, smoking his cigarettes, flipping through the magazines, until the sun rose high above the town.

Chapter Thirty-three

Matthew woke up in familiar surroundings. They weren't the most familiar of recent times, but he remembered them. He had known them for most of his life, since he was four years old. He knew there was a basketball hoop nailed to the wall just below his window. He knew there was a stack of 'Silver Surfer' and 'Daredevil' comics in the closet, along with a soft leather baseball mitt that had started to fall apart at the seams, and an old eight track player which hadn't worked since he had taken it apart for a back fired science project. He had tried to repair it, but never managed to do so. Some of his most comfortable clothes still hung in the closet, the ones that weren't suitable for working in a room full of teen age girls who may have more hormones than was sensible.

It was his own bedroom, and he knew he was home.

A smile spread itself across his face. The room was coming slowly into focus. The red walls had been his choice when he was in junior year of high school. His mother had tried to dissuade him from them, and from the acid green carpet. He had always loved his room. He slowly sat up and looked across to the window. Outside, the blue sky was clear of clouds just as it had always been when he was growing up, perfectly blue.

It was still early, but below him, he could hear his mother moving around in the kitchen, clattering pans. He could smell the bacon already, and knew that it was Saturday morning. He pulled back the bed sheets, and crossed to the closet. His favourite jeans were still hanging there, waiting for him to return to a life that he had very nearly left behind entirely. They were skin tight, faded to a pale indigo. There was a large tear in the left knee, and the ankles were well frayed where he had worn them with boots. They fit perfectly, even though he had been living on fish sticks for months. After he had pulled them on, he turned to the bottom drawer of the dresser. He pulled out an old grey t-shirt. This, too, was skin tight, clinging to his body just the way he wished it to.

Once he had dressed, and combed his shoulder length hair through, he went out into the hallway. Directly opposite, Annie's door was shut. He felt drawn to it, knowing that she was just beyond the white, painted, wood. He moved toward it, conscious of the fact that he was not alone in the house on his side of the door. But as he got closer, he could hear her moving around the room, humming the song that was so strangely familiar to him. He smiled to himself, and rapped lightly on the door.

"Annie?" He called gently. A few moments passed, and she opened the door, smiling out at him. She was dressed in jeans, and a pale blue shirt. Her long hair was plaited, and she was, as usual, stunningly beautiful.

"Good morning." She smiled.

"Good morning. I think I can already hear mom downstairs building us plates of breakfast." He told her. They went downstairs together, and into the kitchen at the back of the house. They found his mother there, dressed, as usual, for any occasion, in other words perfectly. He kissed her lightly on the cheek, and she smiled up at him.

"Well, now, you two sit yourselves down, while I finish fixing breakfast for you." His mother greeted.

They sat at the table across from each other, and his mother placed plates in front of them. It was the same kind of breakfast she had been making on Saturday mornings for as long as he could remember. The plate was covered with eggs, bacon, toast and sausage. There were pancakes in the centre of the table, and he made a move on them before anything else, covering his plate with syrup, and tucking in. Annie seemed to be eating far more sensibly, seeming to restrain herself. There was no way that either of them would need to eat again until mid afternoon.

"We should leave here at about eight thirty. We'll be up at the reservation by about nine that way." Matthew told Annie. She nodded her agreement as she took a forkful of eggs to her mouth. He looked at his wristwatch; it was 7:53.

"Will you be home for dinner, Matthew?" His mother asked him.

"Mom, I wouldn't miss dinner for anything. We won't be with the doc for too long, I guess, and I might just convince Annie to come to Bankie's for a few drinks with Brandon." He replied, hoping that Annie would come, because he rather wanted for Annie and Brandon to get acquainted. "We'll be back early-ish."

"Well, I have a meeting of the Ladies Guild this afternoon, so don't come home too early. Mitsy Williams is coming by to pick me up for my meeting, and I just hate to think what she will say about that hair of yours this time. Dinner will be at seven tonight. By that time, Ben should be back. I know he's desperate to talk to you about how you're doing up there. " His mother told him, refilling the orange juice glass in front of him. As she poured, the radio on the sideboard bristled into action with the news. He could feel himself turning red, knowing that Mitsy Williams had always made a big deal about the appearance of others, when it was really none of her business. A look at Annie showed that she thought it was rather funny, so he dropped his eyes back to the plate, and tried to listen to the radio, instead.

"Good morning, this is the local and state side news. It's Saturday, April 17th, and the time is now eight am. In local news, there was a small fire behind Pringle's this morning. There were no injuries, and the authorities are regarding the fire as accidental. The local Ladies Guild are to hold their annual coffee morning next week, all are welcome. And in state side news this morning, there has been a violent homicide at the 4 star Gasoramma in northern New Mexico. The forecourt cameras showed a light green late model Honda, registered to a young male in Colorado. The authorities have questioned the male in conjunction with the case, but do not feel he is connected to the homicide. At this time, the police have no further leads, but are calling for any witnesses to come forward." The female voice reported. Matthew almost dropped his fork. They had stopped at the very same gas station the night before. He suddenly didn't feel very much like finishing his pancakes, regardless of how good the bacon was. One look at Annie showed him she was thinking the same things as she was.

"That poor boy." Matthew shivered. Annie put down her own fork, and took a drink from her orange juice glass, her face suddenly a little pale.

"Are you all right, Matthew?" His mother asked, looking concerned. "You've gone very pale."

"Ah, well, it's just that we were at that service station last night. It just seems a little weird to hear about a murder taking place there, is all." He replied, feeling a little embarrassed by his own reaction to the news bulletin.

Half an hour later, they were climbing back into the car. Matthew had insisted they drop the roof, letting the sun shine down on them. It was just how he had always loved the car best, gleaming in the morning sunlight. The drive to the reservation was only short, but the roads had to be taken fairly carefully in the large car. He directed her there, knowing the route so well. He had ridden his bike there when he was a kid. When he got the car, he had driven to and from the reservation as often as possible.

"You'll like Brandon, most people do. And I hope you'll indulge us and drive us to Bankie's later." He told her as they were making their way there. A few minutes before nine, they pulled up outside his best friend's house. Brandon was sitting on the porch steps, waiting patiently as ever. Matthew smiled broadly, and called to his friend. "Hey, Brandon!"

"Mattie, how you doing, man?" His friend asked, crossing to the car quickly. "And you must be the student."

"Annie." She smiled, cutting the engine, and offering Brandon her hand. "Pleased to meet you."

"I'm sure the pleasure is all mine. Come on, Dad has had to take a run out quickly, but I'll get you into the hot seat while you wait." Brandon smiled. They climbed out of the car, and followed Brandon into the house. Matthew took a deep breath as he crossed the threshold, remembering the scents of a childhood not entirely his own. He remembered the house as well as his own. It was single storey, built of stone, the walls twelve inches thick. He remembered this house more even than his own when he was back in his apartment.

He knew the house so well. The creaky floorboard in the kitchen, the hole under the sink in the bathroom, the worn rug in the hallway that Brandon's mother had covered with a carpet. Childhood memories of running through the house, being chased by Brandon or one of the other members of their group of friends. More than those, though, he knew the old leather armchair in the study where Annie would soon be sitting. The green leather was softer than butter, rich and supple. He had long been intrigued by all the people who had taken their journeys in that seat. Today he would finally get to see the way it worked, as Brandon led them into the study. "Take a seat, Annie, Matt. I'll go get you some drinks while you wait."

"You sit in that one." Matthew told Annie,

pointing at the green leather armchair. He watched her as she sank into the seat. Brandon left, coming back a few minutes later with two glasses of iced tea.

"Leave the chair alone, Mattie. I know that you and it have a history, but really!" Brandon commented as he came back in. Matthew hadn't even been aware that he had been kneading the leather between his fingers. "He used to sneak in here to do that when my dad was out."

"It's a nice chair." Matthew said defensively. He had the sudden thought that Brandon might be telling this story because he had instantly set his own sights on Annie. But there was no way that that could be the case. "Bran, it will be okay if I stay, won't it?"

"No problems. Dad expects you to be here, anyway. I have to go out for a while, but I'll be back early afternoon." Brandon replied.

"I'm trying to talk Annie into driving us out to Bankie's later, if you'll come with us." Matthew offered.

"Sure, I'll see you back here at about two?" Brandon agreed. A few minutes later, Brandon left, and his father returned. They could hear father and son out in the hallway, discussing something or other. Annie was starting to look nervous again.

"Are you feeling alright?" He asked her, a note of concern in his voice that he could not conceal now that they were so far from the eyes that would frown upon it being there.

"A little nervous." She admitted. "You aren't going to make me walk around like a chicken or something, are you?"

"No, unless you want me to." He teased, amazed that he could do so with such ease. "The doc is a good guy, and a professional. He won't make you do anything, I promise."

"So wise you are, Matthew Wilkins." Came the voice of the doctor from the doorway. "And this must be Annie. Welcome."

"Nice to meet you." Annie smiled. Matthew rose, and shook the doctor's hand. He had always felt at home there, as if the doctor was part of his own family. He took his seat again, and looked at Annie, whose face seemed to be growing more tense by the moment. He wanted to place a protective hand on her shoulder, but he did not have the nerve to do so.

"Shall we begin?" The doctor asked. Annie looked at Matthew, and all he could offer her was what he hoped would be a comforting smile. She turned from him back to the doctor, and nodded. "Alright, Annie, I'd like you to focus on one point in the room, and to concentrate upon that one thing. And keeping that focus, Annie, I want you to listen to my voice. Feel your mind relaxing as it starts to sleep. Further and further relaxing, so that your whole being starts to relax. Your body sleeps while your consciousness remains alert. No pain will come to you physically, you can feel nothing as your eyes fall asleep, your whole body following. Now only your memory is awake. Is this so?"

"Yes." The voice was so different, so far away that he almost didn't recognise it.

"Where are you?" The doctor asked her.

"I'm in the living room. My brother is playing cards with Gerry. Malcolm and Harry are coming this afternoon for tea. Carrie is coming, too, so it's almost like a party. Alex, don't pull Carrie's hair. Alex likes Carrie, I know he does. Oh good, Malcolm's here!" The voice told them. It was not her own voice, but rather that of an English child. However, as Annie continued, the voice grew older. "We're older now. We sit in the tree, just how we used to. Now, though, we are lovers. We would get married, but mummy wants me to marry Harold, dirty little sneak. At least Malcolm is willing to fight for us. Harold won't. He doesn't even have the nerve to be a conscientious objector. He is just getting away with telling them he can't see properly. It would serve him right if they caught him out. But they do have money, and mummy worries about money so very much. It doesn't help now that Alex and Carrie are married, either. Still, never mind, because Malcolm and I are going to run away together and get married on Monday, before he has to leave for the air force." Her voice fell silent for a moment before asking: "What do you mean Malcolm is missing? He can't be missing; we're getting married on Monday. His house was bombed? Are you sure he was in there? Well, maybe he isn't dead, then. The river? No, he wouldn't do that, he loves me, he wouldn't do that…….."

There were tears running down Annie's cheeks, as they listened to her carrying on a conversation with someone long since dead. Who it was, they could not know, but there was one thing that was sure, the man she had loved was dead. Her tears had been flowing silently for almost a minute when she finally spoke again.

"He didn't fall, and he didn't jump. Harold pushed him."

Chapter Thirty-four

"We want to go back, back further. Back, back. Now, what is happening?" The doctor asked. Matthew's own feelings of tension had been steadily increasing.

"It's still raining. It's been raining for days now. The wedding has been postponed because the church is flooded again. I am relieved I must admit. Perhaps now we will be able to convince my parents that this match is wrong. They just don't understand that I can't love Harvey. All the while that I breath, I will love Michael. I will be with him, even if it takes all my days to get there." Her voice trailed off. The stain of the tears was still on her cheeks, but her eyes were now dry.

"What year is it?" The doctor asked, and her face frowned a little.

"Why, it's 1535, sir." She laughed distantly.

"And where are you?" The doctor probed further.

"Well, Scotland, sir, where else?" She asked with surprise.

"I'm sorry, what was I thinking? Of course it's Scotland. So, tell me more about Michael and Harvey."

"Well, I've known them both for so very long. My Michael is very handsome, with dark hair, and friendly eyes. He looks at me as if I am the only girl in the world. When I tell him that, he always laughs, tells me that I may as well be, because he only ever sees me. I have loved him since the first day I met him, which is a very long time ago. When he kisses me, I forget the whole world. I wish it weren't forbidden for us to be together, but if we ever get caught, then it will be the end for us both, I know. They would banish him, and I would never see him again. As for Harvey, he is merely an obstacle that will keep me from a life that I should have. I will never love him, ever."

"So, what are you doing now, then?"

"I'm waiting for Michael. We have to meet in secret, so we wait until it is very late before we are together. I am sheltering under our tree, waiting for him. He is a little late, but that may be because of the rain. I hope he has managed to get away un-noticed, because I miss him when he is away from me. I should really go to find him; at least I will know he is unharmed. I will have to be careful, as the ground is very wet, and I do not wish to be seen unless there is no other choice. I know I can trust you not to tell any other what I have said. If you see Michael, please, tell him that I have gone to find him, that I will come back here for him."

"Of course. Where do you think he is?"

"He may have stopped by the river, he sometimes

does, so I'll try there first. The river is high from the rain. Do you see that?"

"What is it?" The doctor asked, leaning forward in his chair a little.

"No, no it can't be. It isn't possible. Please, lord, no, no! Ahhhh! Ahhhh!" The scream was so loud that it echoed off the walls and around the room. The tears were back, spilling even more quickly this time than they had before. He didn't care what the consequences were, any more, as he reached out, and lay his hand on her shoulder, leaning closer to her than he had dared to do before.

"What's wrong?" He asked, whispering gently in her ear, hoping that it was all right for him to be asking her questions when she was only supposed to be aware of the doctor's voice.

"But I saw you! I saw them lay you in the ground. It isn't possible. How can you be talking to me, Michael? I know that you are dead." She cried softly.

"It's okay, I'm here." He told her, looking down at her, shoulders shaking, tears rolling silently down her cheeks. It had taken less than a second for the words to sink in, and for realisation to spread through him. He felt his arms wrapping themselves around her before he really knew he was doing it. He didn't care anymore, knowing that the doctor had just heard everything that he had. He stroked her hair away from her face, and the tears from her cheeks. He turned to the doctor, without the slightest hint of a smile. "Bring her out of it." He said calmly. "Now, please."

"Of course, Matthew, I understand." The doctor nodded his agreement. Matthew pulled his arms from around her, and sat back in his chair, but continued to look at her, realising that he had been right to talk to her in the first place. As the doctor started to wake her, he realised that he was going to have to figure out exactly what he would say to her when she asked him. He decided that he would have to lie.

Chapter Thirty-five

He wouldn't tell her what had happened. The only thing she had managed to get out of him was that they had not gone back far enough to reach her dreamland. Other than that, he would tell her nothing. Could it really have been that bad? There was a chance that she had said something, of course, something that would have affected him in some way.

They waited a while for Brandon after the doctor had finished with her. When he returned, the three of them climbed into the car, and they started directing her to the place that they described as the best bar in the whole state.

"We used to hang out there when we were in high school. We never drank, of course." Brandon told her.

"Of course." Matthew agreed, laughing. He had

given up the front seat, and now Annie was driving along next to Brandon. She was enjoying the playful interaction between the two of them, but still could not escape the feeling that things were being kept from her. "I swear, as a figure of authority, that I never drank a beer at Bankie's until I was well and truly legally able to do so."

"I don't care, why would I care?" Annie laughed. "You weren't my teacher back then."

"He has always cared a little too much about what he did in the past, and no where near enough about the future." Brandon told her, smiling. "Take a left here. The best thing about Bankie's is that the cops never come anywhere near it except on Sunday nights. None of us could figure that out, until it turned out that the sheriff had a thing for the barmaid who only works on Sunday evenings. That revelation only came to light a little while ago, Mattie, which is no doubt why you have that look on your face. Oh, take the next right. I guess Harry didn't take long to get over that wife of his when she left him."

"You're terrible, Bran! Here we are, Annie. Pull in to the parking lot behind." Matthew announced. They had arrived in front of an extremely run down looking bar. The sign above the door gave the name as Bankwood's Bar, which was obviously how the place had become known as Bankie's. Annie suddenly felt a little dubious about the place, but then again, she trusted Matthew.

"Don't worry, Annie. I can see that look on your face, but trust us. It's not like we brought you to a titty bar." Brandon joked.

"Brandon! Please, no talk of titty bars in front of my students. Brandon wouldn't know where to find a titty bar if there was a big neon sign above it. Besides, there aren't any around here. Not that I frequent them, you understand. Shit! Annie, is there any chance that you could forget everything that I have just said, because if Hathaway ever gets wind of any of that, you know she'll kill me. Mind you, I might manage to impress Ali Rice with that kind of talk. Shit, I give up." Matthew sighed. She could see in the rear view mirror that his face had gone rather red. Annie giggled, but Brandon was laughing loudly. She knew fully well that Matthew Wilkins was way too squeaky clean for that kind of thing. She swung the car into a space in the lot, and cut the engine.

They all got out of the car, and went into the bar. It was almost as dingy inside as it looked from the outside. There was a pool table in one corner, and an old jukebox. The bar was covered in old pictures and flyers for bands that had long since disappeared into the mists of time. The lights were low, and there were a fairly large number of people in there considering the time of day. They managed to find seats around a small table, and settled into them.

"What'll you have?" Matthew asked them both.

"Are you feeling alright, man? Are you really going to buy the drinks?" Brandon asked in disbelief. Matthew nodded yes. "Well then, I will have a beer, thanks Mattie."

"Annie?" He asked, looking directly at her. Even if she hadn't been driving, there was no way she would have even thought of drinking alcohol when she knew she would be alone with Matthew Wilkins.

"Cola, thanks." She replied, smiling a little.

"I will be back as quick as I can. Talk amongst yourselves." Matthew told them, standing up and making his way over to the bar. She watched him as he went.

"I can see how much he likes you." Brandon told her while she was still watching him up at the bar. "He won't admit it, but then again, he's always been stubborn, I guess."

"Okay, I didn't even have to confess to that one, did I? But it's more than him just being stubborn, I think." Annie admitted. "I think he's scared. There are all these rules, you see, and I know they have him freaked out. This would break so many of them, you know? Hell, I'd drop out altogether if I thought it would help anything. Am I really that transparent?"

"No, I just know him very well, and I'm good at reading people. Has he realised he's your match, yet?" Brandon asked.

"I don't think so, even though I knew instantly." Annie smiled. "But I can't tell him. There is no way I can tell him the truth, I wouldn't even know where to start. The worst thing is, he won't tell me anything that I said in your dad's office this morning. I have to think that what I said must be kind of bad. Or maybe, I gave myself away, and he can't deal with it. What if he doesn't feel the same way?"

"It's more likely that he doesn't know whether or not *you* know, and he isn't sure how you feel. I'm afraid that Mattie was always insecure, you know. He was always too bookish at school if you ask me. He basically avoided girls altogether. The fact is, he has one smitten soul over there, and I'm pretty sure that you feel the same, so please, just get on with it." Brandon assured her.

"I just wish I could be sure, though, you know. I wish there was some way to just tell him without saying it in so many words. Maybe if I don't say it, then the rules won't be broken." She sighed. He had finally managed to get the drinks, and was on his way back to the table. If Brandon were right, then she would eventually figure out how they would be together. For now, though, she would simply have to wait.

"Bran, you weren't telling Annie all my dark secrets, were you?" Matthew joked, although she could hear a hint of worry in his voice. She glanced at him for a moment, then back at her glass of soda.

"Only the one about you when you were seven, and you decided that you were……." Brandon started, but his friend punched him hard on the shoulder with his plastered arm. Brandon squealed with mock pain, and Annie laughed. The way they acted together reminded her of Gary and André in years gone by. She hoped that neither of them ever decided they were bigger than the world as her brother eventually had done. Brandon turned back to Annie, and smiled. "Actually, he doesn't have any dark secrets, at least none that I know about."

"And that's the way I intend to keep it, thanks buddy." Matthew grinned.

"How did you two meet?" Annie asked, trying desperately all of a sudden to carry on a normal conversation. For some reason, she had started to feel rather self-conscious that she was sitting in a bar with these two men in the middle of the day.

"He fell off his big wheel in the park." Matthew replied. "Dad went to help, and I had to go along for some reason. We were little kids at the time, not long after I moved here from North Carolina."

"I tried to get rid of him, but he just wouldn't go." Brandon sighed with a smile. "Eighteen years later, and

I'm *still* trying. But in all honesty, life would've been kinda dull without him around."

"And here was I thinking that *I* was trying to get rid of *you*! We went to school together, and he tried to set me up on *countless* dates, with half the girls in our class, that's the half that wouldn't go out with him, or the half that *he* wouldn't go out with, rather. You know, I think I've done enough damage to my reputation for a while, so I'm going to be quiet for the rest of the afternoon if you don't mind." Matthew seemed to be admitting to all his own dark secrets without any assistance from his friend.

"It might be wise." Brandon agreed. "So, how did you two become friends?"

"Oh, we aren't friends, really." Annie felt herself saying rather too quickly. "Sorry, that sounds really harsh, doesn't it? What I mean is, that we aren't friends because he's my teacher, and I draw the line at that."

"She speaks the truth." Matthew agreed, sounding rather annoyed by the fact. "In all honesty, I have to stay professional toward *all* my students, because otherwise, people get annoyed with me."

"So, instead, we are acquaintances." Annie shrugged. She was starting to feel a little uneasy about the whole thing, now. The fact was, she shouldn't be anywhere near there. Finally, she decided to do the only thing she could think of, and excused herself, slipping out of the bar, into the bright afternoon sunlight.

Chapter Thirty-six

"Do you think she's alright?" Matthew asked his friend. He had been wondering this for a while. In fact, it had been bothering him since the doctor had woken her up from the session.

"I think she's more than likely overwhelmed by everything. Wouldn't you be?" Brandon responded.

"Personally, I think she has it kind of easy. She knows exactly who she's looking for. I wish I was so lucky." Matthew grumbled. It wasn't until then, though, that he noticed the look on his friend's face. It was the same look Matthew had been given when he had first told his friend that he was going to be a teacher, the look that told him Brandon already knew. In retrospect, he realised he had never been able to keep anything from his best friend. To be honest, he had never really wanted to, anyway. Now, sitting face to face in the bar, he was as unable to hide the truth as he had ever been. Finally, Brandon gave him the biggest smile Matthew had ever received from him, and he let out a sigh of relief.

"I like her, she's nice. I know what you're worried about, but damn the ethics, man! She is perfect for you." Brandon laughed.

"I can't damn the ethics, though. If I choose Annie, then I have to give up teaching, which is what I thought I wanted to do since I was fourteen, even though I'm not so sure any more. If I choose teaching, then I don't get Annie, who I've waited all my life for, and who I can actually see a future with. If only I could be sure, 100% straight up sure." Matthew admitted, feeling the same insecurities that had followed him throughout his life.

"So where's the problem? You just said you aren't sure you really want to teach, and that you love this girl. So, what if I told you what I know?" His friend asked, leaning forward across the table.

"What *do* you know?" Matthew asked back, leaning forward also.

"I know that while you were up there getting me this rather fine beer, Annie admitted everything, and she's terrified that *you* aren't interested in her. I also know that she just admitted that she would drop out of college for you because of these same ethical problems that you seem to be trying to deal with. I know she thinks she said something earlier that has you worried. I also know that no matter what, this is meant to be, because although she hasn't recognised me, I recognised her right away, and I know that she is right, that time is running out." Brandon conceded. Matthew looked at his friend, realising for the first time that he also had an old soul. It took a moment longer to realise exactly what he had told him about Annie.

"Oh. *Oh!* So now would not be the right time to give up hope, I'm guessing." Matthew grinned. "Actually, she's right, she did say something that gave her away, I just wasn't sure what to tell her about it. We only managed to look at two of her pasts, but I'm pretty sure I ended up dead both times."

"I guess that isn't so good, but you have to trust that everything will turn out right, man." Brandon smiled in his usual laid back style, which would not have been out of place on a spaced out hippy. "She needs to know the truth about what happened to us. Actually, I'd rather like to know myself, from a different viewpoint. I was away almost a day before the quake happened. I have no idea what happened at the end."

"Should *I* have some idea?" Matthew questioned.

"Apparently not, for some reason. Maybe you're supposed to be in the dark until she's ready to tell you. Of course, I may have just put my foot in it. Well, what can they do except to recycle me away from my group? I'd still manage to find everyone. Fate has her way of drawing us together."

"Do I look the same?" Matthew asked, feeling intrigued more now than ever.

"Put it this way, the hair has always been around."

"See, I told my mother I grew it for a reason! She would've recognised me anyway, though, right?" He asked again. Brandon nodded.

"Same way I did, Mattie. Actually, you probably noticed her the same way, by the faint glow she gives off when she's around you. You may not have even realised it was there, but it was her soul reaching out to yours when they found themselves so close together. She glows for you and you alone, though. I watched her get brighter when you came closer. That is sure sign enough." Brandon agreed, and Matthew realised that his friendship with Brandon, which had started so long ago, was less a matter of chance than he had always thought. Looking across the room, he saw that she was on her way back to them. He no longer wanted to divert his gaze from her as quickly as possible. For some reason, he just didn't care anymore whether she realised or not. He finally knew for certain that she was in exactly the same position as he was.

"Well, I know you weren't discussing *my* dirty little secrets, because I only have one that you know about, and it really isn't that interesting." She smiled, pulling her glass of cola toward her. Brandon chuckled, and gave his friend a knowing glance. "Or maybe I really *do* hum in my sleep, and talk, too, and now you've realised that I'm really weird."

"Well, humming in your sleep isn't a crime." Brandon said, not understanding the joke that they shared, but Matthew laughed anyway.

"It's okay, I don't believe you hum in your sleep, anymore." He told her, feeling the intensity of his stare stronger than ever.

"I'm not sure I believe you, Matthew Wilkins, but I'll let it slide." She told him. He knew he was walking a fine line, one that may fall away completely if he wasn't careful. It was at that point he realised Annie seemed to be ringing. She started to look around, then check her pockets. She pulled out a cell phone from her jeans pocket, and looked at the display on the front of it. "Sorry, I should take this, excuse me." She stood up, and flipped the phone open. "Joanna?"

"It's her roommate." Matthew explained after Annie had stepped away. She had moved into a corner of the bar. "She's probably thinking that Annie's been abducted."

"Maybe she has been. Don't tell me that no ulterior motive ever occurred to you for this weekend." Brandon suggested slyly.

"Okay, maybe it did, but it was never going to happen. At least, I didn't think it was. See, you've got me all confused now. Oh, why won't she just tell me? Then I wouldn't have to make up my own mind anymore. She could do it for me." He was starting to grow impatient now.

"Don't ask me!" Brandon shrugged, his hands up in surrender. "All I know is that she's scared. She has a right to be. When she realised that all of the people in her dreams were turning up, she had a right to turn and run for the safety of the hills. The fact that she has embraced so many people means that she is strong. But none of us are *that* strong. Remember that fate is fickle, but that we are thrown together for a reason."

"It just doesn't seem fair." He grumbled, knowing how childish he sounded, even to himself. "Brandon, I'm pretty sure I love this girl."

"Well, it's about time. I've known you for too long, Mattie. I've waited for you to announce that piece of information since I first heard there was a girl having dreams." He was wearing the same smile he had worn on every good occasion during his years, and Matthew couldn't help but smile back. "She won't be on the phone for long, so I'm going to make my suggestions right now. Tell her the truth. She already knows anyway. Tell her you love her, she'll understand. Then, try and figure out what exactly you want to do with yourselves, because I don't think that you will ever be truly happy until you have decided what you want to do with your future. I will continue to despair until you can confirm that you have finally managed to get that girl into your bed."

"Technically, she has been, but I'm guessing that isn't what you mean."

"If you mean that you slept on the couch so that she could sleep in your bed, then no, it isn't. One day, and it will be soon, she will let you touch her as more than a friend, and I'm not too sure you will know what to do. I'll tell you this much, though, she won't know, either." Although Brandon was still talking, Matthew was looking over to the corner where Annie was standing, her back toward the room. He was halfway to remembering what it felt like to hold her, but the thought of touching her was more than he could really bear. Brandon had just mentioned the idea of undressing her, and there was no way he could handle that thought and still look at her. He averted his eyes, knowing that if he did not, it would only make it harder for him later on. "She's coming back."

"Sorry, guys, that was my roommate, Joanna. She's been trying to reach me all day, but obviously I didn't have a signal before. She got home last night, found the word 'bitch' carved into the door, and started to freak out. I left her a note, but she didn't find it right away, so she asked her boyfriend to stay with her, just in case anything else happened. His car got stolen some time during the night. Guess what? He drives a green

Honda, and he spent most of the early hours of this morning talking to cops about a homicide last night. No prizes for guessing what the hell is going on here. I can't believe I didn't figure it out sooner." Annie announced, looking very, very worried.

"He's on his way here. How did he know where to find us?" Matthew asked. He felt suddenly ill.

"I left a few details with Jalena. She spotted me on my way to your place with my bag, and she started asking questions. He must have seen us talking, and figured it out. Oh God, what if he's hurt her?" Annie cried.

"Then Gary will kill him before I get the chance." Matthew assured her. He could see Brandon looked confused, but he didn't have the energy to explain everything to him. All he could manage was to rub his left hand over the plaster cast wrapped around his right wrist. Brandon nodded his understanding. "Okay, I think we should really get a move on, then. Sorry, Bran. We'll be back out to see your dad tomorrow, but for now, I think we should run you home."

Chapter Thirty-seven

"I didn't give her an exact address, because I didn't have one. There's no way he could actually find us, is there?" Annie asked.

They had dropped Brandon back at his house, then started back onto the road. The drive was not far, but it had started to rain, and Matthew had insisted that they drive slowly through the fairly narrow roads. She had been silently panicking about the prospect of Harley finding them since she had started to talk to Joanna.

"He could do. He could find us fairly easily if he wanted to. But I don't think he wants to find us." He sounded as if he was trying to reassure her, but he wasn't very convincing at it. She decided to change the subject.

"I like Brandon." She said, looking straight ahead at the road. The front wipers were going so fast that they seemed to be little more than a blur.

"He's a likeable guy." Matthew commented quietly.

"Are you going to tell me what I said?" She asked, still looking at the road, but wishing that she were looking directly at him.

"Not yet. I have to confirm some facts first." He responded vaguely. She knew he was lying, but there was nothing she could do about it. "Don't worry, you didn't have a fling with JFK or anything."

"Well, isn't that a relief!" She responded ironically. She felt bad as soon as the words left her mouth. "I'm sorry, I didn't mean that. I'm a little nervous is all."

"I know." He nodded his understanding. She suddenly felt the strongest urge to pull over and confess everything to him, but there was no way that she could do so. Instead, they both fell back into silence. When they finally reached the house, they got out of the car, and made a dash for the house now that the rain was really starting to come down. The house was empty, but she didn't feel like being alone with Matthew right then. As he made his way into the kitchen, she continued up the stairs to the bedroom where she was sleeping.

The higher she climbed, though, the less at ease she felt. Something didn't feel quite right. It was nothing that she could instantly put her finger on, but she knew it was wrong. As she reached the door to her room, though, she knew what it was.

The door was open.

"Matthew!" She called, suddenly frozen on the spot. Within a minute, he was at her side.

"What's the matter?" He asked, looking at her

with a mixture of concern and fear.

"I left that door closed, and I don't think your mother would have left it open." She responded, feeling vague.

"You're right. Mom likes everything to be neat, and for private space to stay that way." He agreed. She felt a wave of appreciative warmth run through her. "And that isn't right, either."

"What?" She asked, and followed his gaze. On the carpet, there were a couple of large, dusty footprints. "They aren't mine, and I doubt they are yours."

As she stepped into the bedroom, she could suddenly feel the sensation that had first met her while she had been climbing the stairs, that she now knew was the presence of someone who shouldn't have been there. It was even stronger than it had been before. They didn't linger there for long, but moved instead into Matthew's room. Here again the feeling grew. There was a picture frame on the floor, face down. As Matthew lifted it, he let out a low, long sigh. He showed it to her, and she understood. It was the same picture as the one he had back in his own apartment, except for one thing. Matthew's face had been scratched from it. On the bed, an old comic was lying open. It looked as if it had been simply left by some kid who had been called to dinner, or to play ball. The picture on the open page was of a man and a woman, who were running for their lives.

"Well, if I had any doubts before, I sure as hell don't now. He's found us, Annie." Matthew sighed heavily, sitting on the bed looking a little defeated. He started to laugh, a hollow, cold laugh that was not his own. "You do realise that he is insane, and he has already killed that guy from the service station."

"Of course I do, but I don't think we can do anything about it." Annie shrugged, feeling defeated herself now.

"There is one thing I can do. I'll call Sheriff Cooper. He can at least keep an eye open. For now, though, I suggest we lock the windows and doors. Come on."

Chapter Thirty-eight

The shaking had started to become constant over the past few days. We were preparing for our journeys. As the quakes started coming closer together, I knew that there was no time for our joining to take place.

We prepared quickly and efficiently, only gathering the things that we would need. And in Isis and Fenda, the ships were being completed. They were hurrying to put the huge constructions together.

Alina assisted me as I prepared. Our journey would be long, but one day we would reach our destinations, and be granted the freedom of their lands, greeted into their cultures as if we were their own people.

"Alina, you will come with me, of course. Alim's faithful assistant Grey will also be coming with us." I told my assistant as we continued to prepare.

"I am not permitted to stay behind, or to leave your side. I will remain faithful to you as long as I am able." Alina assured me, pouring perfumed water into a phial before sealing it well with wax.

"We will live in a land where you and I are both free to follow our hearts, where we are not made to live lives that do not hold pleasure for us. You will be free to love Grey, and he to love you." I told her, knowing that the same was also true for me, that I would be free to love Malarchy.

"I wish for that to be so." Alina bowed, and made to leave my chamber.

I knew that within only a few days I would be free. I would no longer have to be confined to the isolation chamber for things outside of my control, for my love for Malarchy. Even as I knew that I would never again see my mother or my father, as they sailed to the west, away from me, I had no fear for my future.

I now also had hope for Brace. It seemed to me that his heart healed quicker than he hoped it would. He understood that Alexis was to join us in our journey, but also was determined to never allow Alexis to again have such a hold upon him, just as I would never have to be close to Haltar against my own will.

Chapter Thirty-nine

The day seemed to have lasted forever. He had ditched the green Honda quickly, knowing it was too risky for him to continue driving it now. The news had been on the radio; even though he knew that there was no way that they would be able to tell that it was him. He knew that the security tapes from the service station would have been distorted, just as the ones from the pool had been. He had never been caught on camera unless he had allowed it to happen.

Instead of the car, he had managed to get hold of a large motorcycle. It was amazing how at ease he felt on the large vehicle, as if this was how he was supposed to be. After all, while his father had still been around, Harley had done very little other than mess around with bikes. They had fixed dozens of them, and he had learnt how to ride when he was still too young to legally do so. He should have looked foolish on the bike. Anyone else his age would have done. But Harley was strong and athletic.

He had managed to find the house easily. There was only one Wilkins listed in the book, a Dr Benjamin Alzar Wilkins. The address was printed next to the name in neat, black letters. When he pulled up outside the house on the bike, he had known without any doubt that the house was empty. He had slipped around the side of the house, and climbed up the wall with ease. There was an open window, and he had let himself climb in through it. It was *his* room, he knew instantly. The walls were bright red, bright enough to hide blood if they needed to, although the carpet wouldn't offer the same service. He had found the picture of Wilkins on his bedside table. Slipping it from behind the glass, he proceeded to scratch the face from it before slipping it back, and dropping it on the floor. Then he had gone to have a look around.

He found her room next. He recognised her flimsy satin pyjamas from her dorm room, and thought just how delicious it would be to get her in those, next to him, both of them dead for the entire world to see. He failed to believe that they weren't for *his* benefit. They sure weren't for hers, because they couldn't offer much warmth on a cold night. Apart from them, there was very little to indicate her presence. The small bathroom that was attached to the room held her toothbrush, and a few little pots of some things or other. This wasn't a place she had been before, though, that much he could tell.

Finally, he went back to the first room, deciding to get a better look, try and figure out what made him so much more desirable to the girl than he had been. It wasn't obvious from looking at his things. He was curious enough to look through the closet, but found very little other than a stack of 'Silver Surfer' comics. He had taken the top one, and flicked through it, finding a picture of a male and a female running for their lives. He had liked the image, and had left it open on the bed. He laughed a little, knowing what their reactions would be when they found it. He almost wished he could hang around to watch.

He couldn't, though. The day was disappearing now, and he knew that if he stayed around for too long, then he would be discovered. He left the way he had entered, leaving the window wide open, and dropping down to the grass below.

Now, once more, he sat above the town where he had spent the night before. The rain that was falling on him was warmer and sweeter than any he had ever known. This was a new form of intoxication, one that he had never felt before, better than even the feeling after he had been with Ali. The only thing that mattered to him now was getting Annie Bouvais and Matthew Wilkins before they ever got the chance to be happy.

Chapter Forty

Annie seemed more apprehensive as she lay back in the soft green leather once again. They had spoken very little about the events of the previous day. He had called the sheriff, and explained that he thought that Harley was after them, and the sheriff had agreed to keep an eye out for him, but that was as far as it went. He had said nothing to either of his parents. Even when his father was re-plastering his wrist (which now meant he could move his fingers) he said nothing about how he had sustained the injury. The real problem was that he couldn't talk to Annie, because his parents were around. Of course, it did mean he managed to avoid her questions about what she had said the day before. He had waited for this long, and he could wait longer if he had to.

"It's alright, Annie." He told her as she leaned

backwards.

"When we're done here, I want you to tell me everything I say, please." Annie demanded, trying to sound like she would not take no for an answer this time. He nodded noncommittally. He knew the truth, and that she knew the same as he did, but he had no idea how he was supposed to tell her. His conversation with Brandon the day before had proved to him that there was a life waiting for him with her if they could just figure out how to get there. He didn't want to ruin that by making the wrong move.

He took a drink from the cold can in his hand. They were waiting for the doctor, while he made a phone call in another room. When he finally came in, Matthew had already finished his drink, and was now starting to feel very nervous, worried about how he would manage to die this time round.

"Are we ready?" The doctor asked. Annie nodded slowly, a gentle smile crossing her lips, then fading. "Alright, then, this won't take long because you are already susceptible. Just relax, and listen to my voice, listen to me as I count backward from 10 to 1, and by the time I have finished, your mind will be released and able to find truths that are otherwise hidden from your consciousness. 10, 9,8,7,6,5,4,3,2,1, and now all that you can hear is the sound of my voice, and the questions that I am asking you. Is this so?"

"Yes." She whispered dreamily.

"Good. Now, we are going back, back in time to where you have been before. Please, tell me where are you?" The doctor asked her.

"Telling my parents that Mary and I are going to get married. They aren't impressed, needless to say.

They want me to marry Helen, because her father has some kind of influence with the drafting board. They don't want me to end up in Vietnam any more than I do, but it makes no difference to me. I love Mary. I always have done, and I'm not going to let the war get in our way. It'll be over soon, and then I'll come back to her. Alice doesn't like Mary, either. Mind you, Alice doesn't like anyone very much. She'll be a bridesmaid, of course. She wouldn't pass up on that chance." Annie gave a little laugh. "Besides, I haven't had the chance to tell them yet, but I got a letter from the draft board this morning. I don't have long before I have to go. I will marry Mary next week, whether they like it or not."

"Don't you fear the fight?" The doctor asked. Matthew knew why the doctor had to ask that question. His own brother had been drafted not long before the end of the war, and never made it back home.

"Not as much as I fear a life without Mary, without love. Of course, Alice has run off to tell Helen about the wedding. I have a feeling that Helen is not going to be happy, because she has a tendency to get a little violent when things don't go her way. I know what she is like. I know what she did to Beth, even if I can't prove it." Her voice up until now had been calm, but suddenly, it grew frantic. "How dare she! Alice, I'll never forgive you for this. You know what Helen is like! I can't believe you just went there and told her. I have to find Mary before Helen does. No, Alice, you've done enough damage already."

"Where are you going to go?" The doctor enquired, his voice so calm that Matthew could barely cope with it.

"Her house, I guess. She should be there. Dad,

I'm borrowing the Corvette. Of course I'll drive carefully." Annie called in the far off voice that was strangely masculine. "What do you mean, Helen picked her up? Did she say where they were going? I have to find her. What's that siren? Oh no, no, not now."

"What happened?" The doctor pressed. Matthew was now so nervous that he had started to bite his fingernails.

"Helen was driving too fast. At least that's what the cops are saying. But how can it be that she's fine when Mary is dead?" She cried. Her breath started to get sharp in her throat, and her eyes suddenly sprang open. She was coughing violently, seeming unable to catch her breath.

"Matthew, go and get a glass of water for Annie, please." The doctor requested, turning to him. He did as he was asked, moving quickly to the kitchen. Brandon's mother was there, doing some baking. She was a small woman, a Navajo by birth, who had married the doctor even though he had less than half a body full of Navajo blood himself.

"Hello, Matthew." She smiled up at him, and handed him a tall glass of water. "For the girl."

"Thank you." He smiled back at her, wondering not for the first time, how she knew things without any hint from anyone. He carried the glass back to the office, where Annie still seemed to be struggling, although her coughing had lessened, and her breathing had become easier. He handed her the water, and she drank from it, gulping it down. "Are you okay?"

"No, no I'm not. I could feel it, I could feel myself dying. It was horrible." She gasped, taking another gulp of her water. It was then that he noticed the shadow of a bruise starting to form in the centre of her forehead. She could obviously feel it, because she reached up, and pressed the centre of the round bruise. "I'm not even going to look at my stomach, I already know what it must look like."

"This has happened before?" The doctor asked, looking a little concerned.

"Yes." Annie nodded, falling back against the green leather with a gentle sigh. "I don't even know how it was happening, although I'm guessing I was shot, quite a few times. Is it normal for me to have no idea what I've just relived?"

"Sometimes." The doctor replied. "Normally if the memories have been traumatic, then the body suppresses them until it is ready to deal with them."

"Then I shan't worry, although I would rather like to know what is happening." She breathed. "I'll be okay, honestly. Don't look so worried, Matthew, I'll be fine. I do know that it wasn't the life that has me troubled, though, because I know there weren't guns back then, so I'd like to go on, if that's alright."

"Of course." The doctor agreed, although Matthew was about ready to protest and take her home right there and then, because even though the bruise on her forehead had already started to fade, he knew it had caused her pain that should have been impossible in her unconscious state. Once more, the doctor began the count back from 10 to 1. Annie's eyes remained wide open, not closing until the very last moment. Now more than ever, Matthew wanted to protect her from these pasts, his pasts, which he was only gaining insight of through her. "Tell me where you are, Annie."

"We set sail this morning, on the good ship that

will take us to the new lands. We are to arrive in the Americas within one week, or so they say. I believe it may take longer. Now that the harbour of New Amsterdam is open to us, many more are heading for these lands. I wish I had not been forced to marry Huntingdon before we set sail, but my father has great influence, and his family is of noble heritage. That is not enough for me. I will never be happy, now. My brother and his new bride may be happy. They will remain in England now, at the estate of Huntingdon's family in Hampshire. The journey would not be so bad for me if Montague were not also on the ship. We have spent too long close to each other for me to simply forget the past. If Huntingdon realised the history between us, then he would not allow Montague to live another day. He has been with the harlot many times, but that is allowed for him, so it seems. He makes to prove that he loves me, but he does not. How could he? His words toward me are harsh; he lacks understanding of who I am.

"It was my parents who forbid me to see Montague, when we were young. They do not care that he is as fine a man as Huntingdon, that he is strong and fine. He does not have the wealth that Huntingdon does, so it makes no difference to them. I will wait for Huntingdon to sleep, after he tries to seduce me. Then I will slip away to meet Montague. He will wait for me until dawn if he has to. I know he will wait for me, as he always did when we were young, when he worked on my father's land with the horses. He is far better at seducing me than Huntingdon will ever be, and I will let him do things to me that would make me blush when I was younger." She was smiling, her cheeks gently blushed pink. Matthew could feel the blush on his own cheeks, and averted his eyes from her completely. "We meet every night for a week, and I am fulfilled in my pleasure, but when the final night of our journey comes, he does not. When the ship is docked, they find him. He has been slaughtered, but I am unable to show how I feel. I cry silent tears for the rest of my days."

The tears were silent now. She made no noise as they slipped down her cheeks, remembering the silent tears that she had wept for the rest of that life. When she turned her head, and raised her hand to wipe away the tears, he knew that she had finally reached the point where her body was ready to accept the memories. Her eyes were open, and she was herself once more.

"Matthew." She whispered. "We have to leave. Harley is coming for us, and he won't stop until he kills both of us."

Chapter Forty-one

"The bitch has a point, you know." The snarl came from the back of his throat, far less husky than he would have liked.

It had not been hard to find them this time, either. In fact, he had simply gone up to the door of the Wilkins house and rung the bell. The woman had been most helpful, telling him exactly where they were. He had introduced himself as Annie's friend, told her some cock and bull story about needing to find her as quickly as possible. He even made out that he could wait, but that he'd rather not if there was another choice. She had given him perfect directions. All he had to do was to get in, which was also very easy. The front door was open.

There was a dark look in Wilkins' eyes. He knew that it was in his honour. The third person in the room was not unexpected now, although he had rather hoped to do this without an audience. The older guy reminded him of a family therapist he'd had to see after their father had died, so very many years before.

"Who are you, and what do you want?" The old man demanded.

"I'm Harley, and I've come for the bitch and her teacher. They aren't going to get away with it, not anymore. They know what I did, I'm guessing. The bitch is too smart for her own good. Shame, I rather liked the guy in the Gasoramma, until he wouldn't give me store credit. I have six bullets in my gun right now." He snarled, pulling the heavy revolver from his pocket. "I need one for the whore back home, so that leaves me with five for right now. Who wants to go first?"

"Me." It was Wilkins who spoke. "You can kill me, but I want you to leave them alone. They won't say anything, you have my word."

"No! No, Matthew, he'll kill us all, just like he always does." The girl cried.

"There's no time to discuss this now, Annie. I get it, really I do. He has to kill me, just like he always does. But not you. It's my sacrifice that saves you." Wilkins told her, not taking his eyes off Harley for even a moment.

"That's not true." The bitch whispered. "Your death always kills me."

"How touching, she can't live without you." He laughed his high, cruel laugh. Annie looked terrified, now. *Good,* he thought, *it serves her right.* The old man wasn't saying anything at all, though. In fact, he seemed to be analysing something. "Hey, you, old guy, do *you* want the girl to live? Does she mean anything to you?"

"Of course she does. I prize all life." He replied. Harley decided to kill him as quickly as possible.

"What is it with the sentimentality that everyone seems to have about this girl? Really, is she so God damned special? Does the sun shine out of her ass? She's hardly even worth the bother, but I hate to get pissed off." Harley continued.

"If she doesn't matter, then let her go, please, Harley." Wilkins begged.

"I'm going to get rid of both of you. How much of a fool do you take me for? I can't leave her alone just because you ask me to." He sniggered. "Now, as I was saying before you decided to get all noble, which of you wants to go first?" Annie was starting to shake now. He watched her, smiling at her fear. He was totally absorbed in what he was doing. A bomb could have gone off beside him, and he would not have noticed it. "You know, my dad gave me this gun when I was a kid. He taught me how to shoot. He was a fool, my father. He had no idea who I really was. Otherwise, he never would have given me this gun."

"Your father gave you the gun? That's interesting. You do look a little tense, though." The old man was talking slowly. Annoyingly so, in fact.

"What are you on about?" Harley asked impatiently.

"I was just pointing out that you look tense. Shooting is hard when you are tense. People tend to miss when they are tense. Are you listening to me, young man?" The old guy asked. Harley felt himself nodding, but wasn't quite sure why. He was starting to feel a little hazy. "Good, because I just want you to listen to my voice. Focus upon your target, and keep that focus, but all the time keep on listening to my voice. You should start to feel your mind relaxing, more and more until your body starts to follow it into slumber."

The voice had now become so distant that it was almost as if it were a dream voice. His eyes had closed, even though he was trying desperately to keep them open.

"Harley, you don't want to hurt us. You and I are going to go for a short drive. When we reach our destination, you will give a full and truthful confession of everything that you have done, about what occurred at the Gasoramma the night before last, about anything else you may have done wrong of recent times." The voice was talking to him from such a distance that he wasn't sure why it had such control over him, or why he would carry out what was requested of him, even if the consequences were great. "Do you understand me, young man?"

"Yes." It didn't even sound like his own voice, but he knew it was.

An hour and a half later, Harley found himself handcuffed to a wooden bench, with absolutely no idea how he had got there. All he knew was that he had just told some guy every bad thing he had done since he was seventeen. It would be enough to keep him locked up for a long while. The worst bit was, he knew that now he had admitted his crimes, he would be well and truly visible in the security tapes.

"Thanks, Doc." It was the voice of an old man; the old man coming out of the office marked Sheriff H J

Cooper.

"No problem, Hank. He was going to shoot Matt and his friend, and probably me, too." The other guy responded.

"Matt Wilkins? Is he back in town?" The sheriff asked.

"Yeah, but I don't think he'll be around too long. Him and his friend have some stuff to work through." The old doctor commented. "Seems like he and she may be soul mates."

"Well, that *is* good news. I always wondered when he'd finally settle down."

Harley didn't say a word. He couldn't find any that explained what had happened to him. He was simply left to sit there, and wonder where it all went wrong.

Chapter Forty-two

She had only called to find out how Jalena was. She hadn't expected to have her call answered by her good friend, Gary.

"Hey, Annie, there was an accident. Well, it wasn't really an accident. That guy, Harley, broke in here and attacked Jalena. She's alright, but he really scared her." Gary told her.

"That's why I called. Look, Harley came down here, and tried to attack us. I won't be back tonight, after all." She called back to him.

"Where are you, anyway? Jalena said something about a field trip with Mr. Wilkins. How come I didn't know about it? I'm in your class, and I'm pretty sure I'd remember hearing about it." Gary questioned her.

"That isn't exactly the truth, but the lie was

necessary. Trust me, I'll explain everything when I get home. For now, I'm where I need to be." She responded. "By the way, why are you still at Jalena's? Did you finally ask her out?"

"Yes, and damn your brother and his ideas about her. We're going out tonight. She's leaving the spotty teenager in charge especially for me." Gary confided. She could feel her smile growing across her face. She wished she could be with him, but knew that she had enough to do before she could leave for home.

"That's great, sweetie. Have a lovely time, and I'll see you tomorrow." She smiled. They exchanged good byes, and she ended the call. She scrolled through the names, and found the number for the frat house. It rang a couple of times before her brother answered it.

"Hello?" His voice came through the air to her.

"Andrew, it's Annie. I just called to say I won't be home this evening after all. I have to stay down here and answer some questions. Harley turned a little nasty, and tried to kill me. I'm fine, but he's been arrested. You might want to let your girlfriend know." She told her brother, finally giving up the ridiculous name he had given himself so many years ago.

"That's my fiancé, Annie. I'm not sure what she will do with that information, but I'll let her know." He responded.

"Did I just hear you right?" She squealed with pleasure.

"Yeah, this afternoon." She could almost hear his smile coming through the line. She congratulated her brother, then switched off her cell phone. She held it between her palms, a smile spreading across her own face. It was the smile that knew her life was finally on the right course. The smile that knew he understood.

"Is everything alright?" Matthew's voice came from behind her. She was standing next to the car, which was the only place she had managed to get a signal on her cell phone. She turned to look at him, and nodded.

"Better than ever, I think." She grinned. "But I think we need to talk."

"Yeah. Come on, Mom is in the den with a group of Ladies Guild women, who would probably try to pin me down and cut my hair if they saw us. Let's go to the back yard." He agreed, and led her down the side of the house to the back yard. They sat side by side on the back porch steps. Now, sitting next to him, she was almost afraid of what she was going to say. In the end, he started for her. "Annie, I'm not sure where to start, you know. I've never been good at this, probably because I've never really had any practice. The truth of the matter is, I have no idea about any of this, except that for some reason we have history."

"That's one way to put it." She smiled nervously.

"Well," he continued. "It's like that song. I have no idea how we both knew the song, but something tells me it belongs to us, that somewhere along the line, you have always sung those words for me. I think I must have known that a long time ago, even before Brandon told me what you told him in the bar. I knew the first time I saw you that there was a link between us. I just didn't know what it was. Brandon says you glow, but I have no idea whether that's true or not. It might explain why I noticed you the first time. But I didn't know what to do about it. I was scared, I guess. I think I probably still am a little."

"I know."

"And then I realised that there were so many things that stood in our way, so many rules that we couldn't over come. I gave up ideas that we could ever be more than friends, and even that wasn't a likelihood at one point. That day, when I first spoke to you, all I could think was that I had at least made contact with you. I'd been trying to figure out how to do it for ages. I even toyed with the idea of holding you back to discuss something or other, but I didn't have the nerve. But after that, it didn't help just making contact, any more. I wanted to be near you more than ever. Then, when I got talking to you, and you told me all your dreams, I thought that I might have lost everything. She's looking for her soul mate, I thought; great, just my luck. I was so unhappy for a while. I even thought that Gary Hutchins was in my way at one point."

"Ah! The amazing car revving trick! We did wonder what that was all about."

"I was in a bad mood after that. Then we seemed to be getting on so well. We were talking a lot, and even though you seemed to be getting all worried about stuff, and I was getting worried about stuff, neither of us seemed to give up on being friends. And I *so* wanted for us to be friends. Actually, all I wanted was to be around you. You had me terrified after that day when you passed out, and devastated when you bit my head off when you weren't sleeping. All I wanted was to tell you everything."

"So, what is it that you want to tell me now?" She asked, finally feeling a little more playful than she had done in a long while.

"That I love you. I know, it seems quick for me to be saying that, but it has been all I could think about for weeks. Actually, it's all I could think about since the first time I saw you. I'm not sure how the world treated us in the past, but I know that we have been here before. I promised I would tell you what you had said, and I'm not sure whether I still need to, but I died at least four times for loving you. At least one of those times we were very close to each other. I think I may be turning a little red right now because I'm thinking about really, really bad things to be thinking about doing with you, who I've been trying to avoid thinking about that way for months, so I'll apologise for the fact that I'm a bit of a prude.

" Brandon thinks it's hilarious that I've never slept with a girl, but to be honest, I never found one that I wanted to sleep with. Not that I'm expecting for you to do that with me, unless you want to. We can't really, anyway, because we have to figure out how I'm going to get out of being a teacher first, and then, I don't know, maybe I'll have to marry you, or subject you to months of fish stick sandwiches, or something. I don't know all the answers yet, or all the right steps. I'm sure Brandon will tell me how it all works. He seems to know everything. Actually, he may even have been around for us a few times before, if I understand him right. I know I'm turning even redder right now, because I just realised I'm going to have to ask my best friend for advice on how to, well, you know. Don't laugh; I can see you're just dying to. The problem is, I still don't know what we are going to do."

"As I told Brandon, I'd drop out for you."

"I'm not going to ask you to do that. Actually, I'm the one who's going to drop out. Don't look at me like that!" He cried, as the smile she had been wearing turned to a look of slight fear. "You and I both know that I don't belong there. Mitchell has been setting my lesson plans for weeks, while Hathaway seems to think I have everything under control. I don't even know why I wanted to be a teacher, but I think it was fate's way of leading me to you."

"Well, we are soul mates, aren't we?"

"I reckon so, Annie."

"And you really would've died to save me?"

"In an instant. I'm rather glad I didn't have to, though, because I've rather been looking forward to kissing you, Annie Bouvais."

"Well, that's good, because I've been waiting. "Just as long as I don't get shot again, I don't care. You know, every time that you died, I gave up living, too. I was cast out of my clan for Witchcraft, you know, because I was haunted by dreams of you, but not *that* you, this you. I gave in and lived my life with a man who I detested, who raped me every night for twenty years, because I couldn't prove he killed you. I went to Vietnam, even though the draft board told me I didn't have to after you died, because life didn't mean anything to me anymore. I have loved you forever, and I'll do anything to stay by your side." She smiled, feeling such relief that things were finally clear to her, now. There was just one thing missing, now. "Of course, there is one more past I need to know about, first, the one I came here to find out about in the first place."

"I'll call the doctor in a minute." He was grinning again, as he slid closer to her, and slipped his arm around her shoulders. He kissed her gently on the forehead, and she felt suddenly happier than she had in days. When he pulled his arm away, and stood up, she felt empty, as if she was nothing without him now. When he returned a moment later, and grabbed her hand, she felt electricity flood through her. For a moment, she was even sure she could see him glow. He pulled her up behind him as if he was unwilling to leave her ever again. He led her back into the house, and made her stand beside him as he called the doctor and asked him to make a house call. He was acting like a teenager, and she couldn't help but join him in his joy. It was all she could do to keep from hugging him as he spoke into the phone. "He'll be here in a while. Come on, I want to show you something."

"Okay." She agreed as he pulled her up the stairs and into his bright red bedroom. The warmth of the room was intense, and she felt instantly at home in it. She waited as he looked through several drawers until he found what he was looking for. He handed her the piece of paper he had been looking for. It held a picture, drawn in pencil, shaded perfectly to give dimension and definition. It was her own face, as she had known it as a child. "It's me."

"I know. I drew that when I was fourteen, believe it or not. How anyone can doubt that fate exists, I'll never know. I've known you all my life, Annie." He whispered. "You and I are meant to be together. That's the only thing I'm sure of now, that and the fact that I love you."

Down stairs, the sound of the doorbell resonated around the hallway. She could hear Matthew's mother open the door and let the doctor in. She sent him upstairs, and Annie realised she was finally going to get to know her oldest past.

Chapter Forty-three

He knew she needed him now as she lay back on the bed in the white guest room. He lay next to her, his arm around her, and she rested her head against his shoulder. He had told her he loved her, and it was true. He had loved her forever.

"Alright, Annie, you know how this goes now. You are relaxing once more, further and further you are relaxing, going back further than you have ever been before, back to the beginning of your very being. Tell me now where you are." The doctor hypnotised her.

"I am leaving home for the last time. The home temple is now deserted apart from Malarchy and I who have to stay behind. As the daughter of our emperor, I have no choice but to carry out his will. Malarchy was not supposed to stay, but he would not leave me. He knows as I do that by the time the sun sets it may already be too late for us to make it to Isis and to safety. The quake will be here before the night is through. We have no more time. Everyone else has gone, now. There is no one here to see us, no one to tell what we are doing. My beautiful city of Aqui Milam is left to ruin. My land will fall into the sea. I will miss this land."

"Where is your land?" The doctor asked her.

"In the middle of a great ocean. To the west, there is a great distance before the land, which is green and plentiful, with great forests full of trees. To the east, the land is closer. The narrow passage will open up to let us through, and we will be welcomed into the land where the earth is dust. The other places will not accept us. Malarchy and I are to go to the east, and we will leave for Isis as soon as the sun sets. It is not far, but we will have to hurry. Malarchy is trying to calm me by singing our song, but he knows so few of the words. I have sung it many times for him, but he never remembers it all."

Matthew realised that he was singing the words that he could remember, humming when he could not recall what they were. Annie's face was smiling.

"Do not worry, you will remember them some day, my love. I think the sun is now setting, and we may now leave here forever. Come, we must hurry." She breathed gently. "What was that?"

"What was what?" Matthew asked.

"A rustling, the sound of breaking twigs. It is a sound I know, the sound that Haltar made the day he wounded Brace." She replied.

"But I thought he was gone." Matthew told her, knowing for sure that his soul was the one that she was talking to somewhere in their pasts.

"He has come to avenge the harm he thinks we have done to him. Come, we must leave here before he can harm us. It is time to leave Aqui Milam. Do you feel the ground shaking? This is stronger than the others. This is Niall's quake. We must get to Isis before the boats set sail, or we will be left here forever. Run with me, Malarchy, please run. Alim and Kylin wait for us. If I don't get there, then Alina will have to stay also. Please, don't let us be too late. I can see the lights, but I hear Haltar calling for help. He has fallen; he cannot get up, Malarchy. Please, keep running; we are so close now, just run. We cannot stop, there is no time." She gasped. She sounded out of breath and confused as she went on. "I am sorry, Alexis, but Haltar cannot join you. He fell and was lost to us. He destroyed himself just as we destroyed our land and ourselves. We have angered the gods with our actions and our wrong beliefs. We have destroyed each other, and ourselves just as Niall predicted we would. We have lost our land, and those we care most about."

"Tell me what you are doing now." The doctor probed.

"We are on the boat." She was calm once more. "Alexis will not believe that Haltar is gone, but Brace is more gracious than I have ever known him. In a few days, we will reach the land to the east. I had no time even to say fair well to my parents. Neither did Malarchy, but we are together, and will be forever now. We may be joined now that Haltar is no longer with us. I may be joined with anyone I wish."

"Then you are free?" Matthew whispered.

"We are free, my love, we are free, finally. We may follow our hearts." She was smiling.

"Then it is time to come back to the now, Annie. Hypnosis is little more than the relaxation of the mind. To reverse the process, we must wake the mind and make it sharpen. Your mind is waking now, Annie, slowly waking from its unknowing state. Your mind is clearing, and your focus is sharpening, and now you are awake." The doctor soothed slowly, bringing her back to full consciousness.

"How do you feel?" Matthew asked her anxiously, looking at her nervously.

"Happy. So happy. Thank you doctor, so much. I can dream again now. Thank you for solving the mysteries of all my pasts." Annie smiled.

"That is my pleasure, Annie, and my job. This is for you. My wife has been making it for months especially for you, or so she says." The doctor told her, handing her a large, flat box. She opened it, and gave a gasp at the contents of it. She held up the large dream catcher, and watched it swaying gently in the air. It was almost identical to his own, with gold-fringed feathers. The pieces of turquoise and silver that had been threaded onto the structure were in the shape of hearts.

"Thank you." She whispered, smiling.

The doctor made his farewells, and left them. Annie curled closer to him, and he breathed in her fragrance, sweet and warm like summer time, a fragrance that he had known for as long as he could remember.

"You can't leave me, Matthew Wilkins. How will I cope if you leave me? You're the only person I have who knows everything, about all of this. Not to mention the fact that I would really miss you, and that I've waited almost six thousand years to be with you again. We made it to the new lands together that time, but we've been parted ever since, forbidden to even speak to each other. If you leave me, I'll fall apart, Matthew. I will fall away to nothing, and I don't think I'll ever get fixed again." Annie frowned solemnly.

"I won't leave you, I promise. I'll find a way to be with you. I'm going to take care of you, Annie." He promised her. "We're on to something good here, you know."

"I know we are. There wouldn't be any life if I didn't have you. I never want to let go of you. You have no idea how long I've been thinking that." She admitted.

"I think I have some idea. I even shouted at myself once because I couldn't just tell you what was going on inside my head. And you know something else? I'm never, ever, going to let you go." He told her. He pulled her tightly into his embrace, folding his arms around her, and searched for her lips with his own.

As they kissed, he knew that he had caught her. Just as the dream catcher of legend caught the bad dreams of the world, he had managed to catch the dreams of the one he loved, the dreams that had brought them together. He knew right then, as the sun shone across their entangled bodies, that this time they truly would live happily ever after.

Soon to come from the same author

Cats eyes

High on a cliff over looking the pacific, stands Tarot house. Catalina Tarot has lived there very happily for her entire life, but this summer, things are going to change for her forever. The arrival of summer guests brings Guy Marin, the mysterious young man who keeps his thoughts to himself, even if he doesn't realise it. As the long hot days of their summer together dwindle, Cat and Guy find their way to each other, but their happiness is not meant to last.

Elixir of Life

In a tall house in San Francisco, the old man sits and waits. At the same time, Electra Phillips tries her hardest to keep going toward her Olympic dreams. Then there is Vagan Elison, who is simply trying his hardest to stop the pain that keeps coming back. When Vagan and Electra meet, their lives become connected. But who is the old man? Even more importantly, why does he want to use these two lives for his own gain? The answers will all become clear in time, but will it be too late by then?

Glistening Asphalt

Audrey Dale has an unusual life. She has a younger sister who is in a mental hospital for something she grew out of ages ago.
She has been sleeping with her stepbrother, Oliver, for three years. Her other stepbrother, Frankie, is in love with her, and involved with the mafia. All just a normal day in Red Bank, New Jersey, huh? But as things go from unusual to downright scary, where will Audrey's heart lead her?

www.ingramcontent.com/pod-product-compliance
Ingram Content Group UK Ltd.
Pitfield, Milton Keynes, MK11 3LW, UK
UKHW021319180426
11947UKWH00015B/1313